About the Author

Eugene Tossany lives in the United States, with two of the quasi-fictional characters from The Down Syndrome Superhero series. She enjoys meshing together ancient research with modern scientific discoveries and an active imagination. As a disabled veteran, and mother of a special needs child, Eugene has a unique perspective about life, survival, and the desire to thrive when giving up seems like such an attractive option. She credits her tenacity to a strong upbringing, in a large family of vivacious personalities.

www.downsyndromesuperhero.com
www.downsyndromesuperhero.co.uk

Down Syndrome Superhero 3

Eugene Tossany

Down Syndrome Superhero 3

Olympia Publishers
London

www.olympiapublishers.com
OLYMPIA PAPERBACK EDITION

Copyright © Eugene Tossany 2023

The right of Eugene Tossany to be identified as author of this work has been asserted in accordance with sections 77 and 78 of the Copyright, Designs and Patents Act 1988.

All Rights Reserved

No reproduction, copy or transmission of this publication may be made without written permission.
No paragraph of this publication may be reproduced, copied or transmitted save with the written permission of the publisher, or in accordance with the provisions of the Copyright Act 1956 (as amended).

Any person who commits any unauthorised act in relation to this publication may be liable to criminal prosecution and civil claims for damage.

A CIP catalogue record for this title is available from the British Library.

ISBN: 978-1-80074-522-3

This is a work of fiction.
Names, characters, places and incidents originate from the writer's imagination. Any resemblance to actual persons, living or dead, is purely coincidental.

First Published in 2023

Olympia Publishers
Tallis House
2 Tallis Street
London
EC4Y 0AB

Printed in Great Britain

Dedication

I dedicate this book to the small veteran community where I volunteer. We make the world a better place one day at a time.

Acknowledgements

Thank you to the medical staff for keeping me whole, intact, and persevering.

Chapter 1

The leaves crunched under my bare feet as I walked to the pier for a sunset night cap. I sipped my hot apple cider carefully, but still splashed droplets on my scarf. I was always challenging myself to walk and drink at the same time. Usually, the beverage was the undefeated champion, much to my chagrin.

Although the sun was still bright, there was a deepening chill in the air, carried by a waft of damp moss. I eased myself into a wicker seat with foam cushions. The cushions were a dark grey, and harmonious with the autumn backdrop. The river water was rippling from east to west, deep blue and secretive. Like old friends, we sat in each other's silence, enjoying the change of seasons.

After some untold amount of time, I exhaled a guttural sigh, releasing decades of angst. Our story had finally ended. My old bones were weary but strong. My heart was fulfilled and retiring. I could tell the spirit and soul were ready, and had probably been ready since before my body advanced in age. These small comforts, and intimate retreats with nature, were the highlights of my regimen – soothing the aches and pains of a boisterous life.

Today was one of those days where the mind begged to be let free. I sat in silence with my thoughts that were starting to take shape, amidst a jumble of memories and nostalgia. It was difficult to express normalcy after a lifetime of supernatural adventure. Where were my thought clouds leading me and was I ready to bramble down memory lane?

Eventually, a whisp of forest magic took hold of my attention. I remembered the first visit to Yellowstone Park, where our intact family made a lifelong friend. It was one of the most pivotal nights of my and Earth's existence, and yet, it was not often spoken of.

Some seventy years ago, the self-made camping area had welcomed us with a balance of tranquility and energy. There seemed to be a certain wisdom flowing out of the earth. I did not realize it at the time, but the wisdom was infusing our speech, guiding our conversations and probably our thoughts. Everything had been so coordinated. When we left that area, we put a universal placeholder on a specific point in time.

I matured beyond my age, even though it took some years before the physical effects were felt. I fared better than others, I pondered, with a slight frown. There was so much that happened within a short amount of time. I was not sure if any of us were prepared. Opal tried so hard to fill those knowledge gaps with clear instructions and guidance.

At the thought of her name, I squeezed my cup, in a moment of fond recollection. Opal. I felt the bulge rise in my throat and the familiar sensation of emotional suppression.

Chapter 2

When the Crow found us, we were in the middle of planning our subversive attack against the Sashimi. We had each been given a piece of the proverbial puzzle. The details of that strange encounter were as clear as a Rocky Mountain day, right down to the color of my socks. I should know because that was the last thing I looked at before my face connected with the floor. As if remembering the aftermath, I reached up and touched my slightly crooked nose. The gesture brought back all the remembrances, including the narrative from those who witnessed the Crow's attack. I closed my eyes and allowed the memories to surface.

My mind drifted to that fateful autumn day when the Crow scratched my hand, setting in motion a sequence of unforgettable events. As I remembered, after I hit the ground, the Crow began to speak. I could hear him now, as I embraced my apple cider, shivering at the distant echo of his voice. The Crow turned out to be one of those villains who loved explaining himself before acting.

On that eventful day, the Crow made his appearance and said, "It is not poison flowing through her blood. It is dark matter dampening her DNA. Listen closely to my instructions and she will live." His voice sounded strained and scratchy.

"You are in no position to make demands," said Opal from her elevated stance on the ceiling beam.

The Crow tilted his head and adjusted his posture to stand at his fullest height. He was about one and a half feet tall with a combined wingspan of three feet. I had no idea how he stayed hidden in the garage. He looked down at my mom and dad who were pulling me up from the floor and dragging me to the area behind our kitchen island. His gaze shifted to Long Shadow, who was in a defensive position on the opposite side of the dining table.

"I know you," said the Crow with cold eyes. "You have something that belongs to me." The Crow curled one of his wings in toward his body and started to pull at an invisible thread. A dark line of shifting atoms streamed from Long Shadow's upper torso, startling him and causing him to swat at the air. He grasped at what appeared to be dark matter leaving his body.

"What is this!?" he exclaimed.

"You've been holding on to a key for me," the Crow said with deliberate certainty. Opal was getting ready to leap into action when he lifted one of his dark wings and shot at her with a dark substance, like what had hit Long Shadow. Opal momentarily tumbled from the ceiling and caught herself midair.

"Alana, Oliver, Long Shadow, I'm so sorry I will not have time to explain. Get ready to fight!" Opal, who was significantly smaller than the Crow, flew at him with amazing speed. She opened her beak and sang a varied chorus as she fluttered around his head. The Crow swatted at her with his free wing and missed his mark.

The entire room moved sideways and began to blend with an alternate dimension. The walls and floor evaporated, making way for a bombardment of red color.

They were back in the ruby forest, much to the Crow's surprise. In fact, their exact location baffled him.

"How did you know we were here?" the Crow asked. He was no longer standing on the chandelier and was gripping at a nearby tree. He was too heavy, and the branch snapped, dropping him to the ground. Opal knew they needed to act fast.

"Now! Capture him!" she shouted from above us. Dad understood and jumped onto the Crow's large body. They struggled, rolling around on a bed of red grass and dirt. The Crow used his dense wings to render serious blows at my dad's neck and face. Feeling the brunt of the impact, my dad loosened his grip and the Crow escaped. He shot up and circled above. He quickly launched at Long Shadow, gouging his right shoulder and screeching a hideous noise, probably notifying the hiding Sashimi.

"Alana, help!" My dad's voice sounded muffled as the Crow swooped in and covered his mouth. My mother was already in motion and leapt at the Crow. She grabbed one of the Crow's wings and wrestled him to the ground. She drove her knee into the Crow's chest, and I could hear cartilage breaking. The Crow screamed and then clamped his beak onto my dad's arm. Long Shadow stepped in, grabbed the Crow's beak, and quickly jerked his head to the side. The Crow's neck snapped, and his body went limp.

"Pick him up, quick!" yelled Opal. "We need to get back to the cabin before the Sashimi realize we're here. Bring him with us." She motioned at the Crow's stiff corpse.

"I've got him," said Long Shadow. He knelt and grabbed a fistful of feathers, slinging him onto his back and using the black wings as backpack straps. Opal nodded her approval and sang us into our dimension. We 'landed' in the living room, under the chandelier. A quick scan of the room and Opal confirmed my sleeping self, still unaware of what occurred.

"That was really close," said Opal, with a noticeable shudder. "When we have time, I'll tell you what he's capable of, and how acting fast was the only feasible option. The Crow has fought in many battles and is a seasoned warrior." She glanced at his body, sprawled on the floor, relishing the fact that he was dead.

Long Shadow followed her gaze, chuckled, and then grimaced, tenderly touching his shoulder. "I'll be right back," he said. "I'm going to find a towel that I can apply to the gaping hole on my shoulder." He exited the living room, with droplets of blood splattering along his path.

"Alana, and Oliver, Josie's in a deep sleep but I can easily reverse her damage. It's you, Oliver, that I'm worried about. You're the protector and they're trying to inflict damage. Yet they're no match for you and me. If I spend a little more time and energy on you then you will be ready for the next part of the journey."

My mom sat on the couch and Dad sat next to her. He was winded, gasping for air, and bleeding from where the Crow bit him. She gently touched his arm while searching the room for material that could be used as a tourniquet. His breathing calmed when he realized what his wife was doing. He clumsily removed his shirt, wincing as the material grazed the wound. Alana helped him wrap the exposed skin and tie the shirt to stem the flow of blood.

"Let me have a look at that." Opal made her way over to the couch and sat on Dad's leg. "The Crow's saliva is venomous. My concern is that we still do not know the extent of Oliver's illness from the portal attack, when he held off the Sashimi. How were you feeling this morning when you woke up?"

"I still felt woozy, but I figured a cup of coffee could cure me," Dad responded.

"Did the Sashimi hit you with anything, like a lightning bolt or invisible energy?" Opal inquired.

"Not that I could see, but I do remember feeling some kind of energy wave that was concentrated on my chest." Dad rubbed his chest as he spoke.

"Aha, sounds familiar. Let me use the black stone to drain the poison from your arm, first. Then, I'm going to put you to sleep and sing healing into your body. Those energy blasts tend to make the insides feel scrambled." Opal flew upstairs and plucked the black stone from Josie's backpack. She set it on Oliver's knee. Next, Opal focused her efforts on a lovely tune, coaxing the dark matter to extract itself from Dad's arm. It streamed out in condensations of black liquid, pausing midair, as if realizing it was no longer dancing inside a vein. Opal opened her beak and breathed a soft tuft of air that evaporated the dark liquid.

"That part was easy," Opal said, "but finding the hidden vibration in your husband's chest and reversing the damage ... well, that will be a little more difficult." Opal stepped back from the black stone and then flew back upstairs. This time, she plucked the yellow stone and set it on the table.

Dad managed a weak smile and said, "Would this be an appropriate time to request you awaken me when it's all over and the Sashimi have been defeated?" Mom held his hand and smiled, racking her brain for the melody to the 80s song Dad inadvertently mentioned. When she thought of the song she crooned, "Wake me up before you go- go…"

Dad laughed, recognizing the *Wham!* song, and asked, "Remember that was the last night we went camping in Big Sur? We were up drinking and renaming the stars with your attributes and personality traits. I believe we named a galaxy *Glistening Navel*, right before we sang ourselves to sleep."

Mom tilted her head back and chuckled, "How could I forget? I was a beer lightweight on our expedition. Everything made me laugh and the world seemed so full of optimism." They exchanged glances with loving nostalgia, temporarily forgetting the present circumstances.

Opal tilted her head, in her infamous '*what are these knuckle heads talking about*' gesture. She cleared her throat and whimsically said, "Oliver, go ahead and lay down so I can sit on your chest and sing you to sleep. I realize you're an adult so spare me the jokes about tucking you in and singing you a lullaby."

Mom and Dad laughed in unison. "Touché," Dad responded as he stretched himself on the couch.

Mom's face grew serious. "Opal, how much longer can we keep this up? The Sashimi have been attacking us every step of the way. Our bodies are worn and Josie's still passed out."

"Yes, dear. And you also have me – your guide, your healer, and your friend. I would say that in the scheme of things, a few body aches and bloody noses are a small price to pay for saving the universes."

Mom spluttered, "The Sashimi didn't just cause body aches, Opal, they terrorized us."

Opal remained silent a few seconds and then said, "Let me put Oliver to sleep and remove the energy arrow. Then, we can regroup."

Chapter 3

About forty minutes after Opal started the 'bad' energy drain, my dad roused from slumber. He was drenched in sweat – his body fighting the Sashimi's grip on his very soul. He screamed twice, during the extraction process.

Opal was aware that his body felt as though it were being torn in two pieces. She could empathize, as she, too, was once wounded with an energy blast. The gold universe hummingbird came to her rescue, similar to what Opal was doing for Oliver.

Oliver opened his eyes, relieved that he was still alive. My mother, and her excellent timing, couldn't hold back another jab, "Welcome back, Oliver. Now you know what it feels like to give birth." She pursed her lips, waiting for Oliver's reaction.

He smiled and said, "Women are superheroes."

"Actually, Josie's our superhero. Alana and Long Shadow, can you please help Oliver from the couch and put Josie in his place?" Opal was quick to resume her life-saving efforts.

Long Shadow had fashioned a belt around the towel, fastening it to his shoulder. His left arm was still maneuverable so, he reached under Josie, and lifted her with Alana's help. They clumsily set her onto the couch, stretching her legs and putting her hands on her stomach. Alana stepped back and said solemnly, "She looks eerily like a corpse." To push the hideous thought out of her mind, she reached down and ruffled Josie's hair, playfully.

Opal took her position on Josie's chest. She sang her healing tunes as they watched the liquid dissipate from her body. Oliver furrowed his eyebrow at the sight of Josie's swollen nose. He waited until the dark matter was gone and Josie opened her eyes.

"Opal, can you repair Josie's nose? She might have a hard time breathing if it's really swollen." He reached down and held Josie's hand. "Welcome back, sweetie."

"What'd I miss? You guys look like a bunch of ex-fight club members."

"We destroyed the Crow and we're now in healing mode," Alana said as she gestured to the ground, where the Crow was still reduced to a pile of feathers.

"Holy Moly!" I exclaimed. I was getting ready to say something humorous when Opal swatted my nose with her wing and sang an 'E' sound.

"Ouch! What'd you do that for?" I reached up and tenderly touched my nose, which was no longer hurting or swollen.

"Just a little magic to reduce the nose swelling. Although, there's nothing I can do about the shape." Opal said.

I looked at her quizzically. "What's wrong with the shape?"

My mother intervened and responded, "It's a little crooked, but still cute as a button. Consider it a battle scar."

"Who's next?" Opal asked with a twinge of humor. She stared at Long Shadow, admiring his make-shift bandage.

Long Shadow visibly cowered. "If you hit my shoulder,

then I might pass out."

Opal laughed. "Such a rugged and whiny crew, eh?" She flew onto Long Shadow's good shoulder. "Remove the towel so I can get a better look."

Long Shadow obliged and removed the bloody belt and towel.

"Ew, that's a nasty gouge. Let me see what I can do. Just hold still so I can put my beak at the cusp of your ear." Long Shadow remained still, smiling a little as Opal partially placed her beak inside his canal. It was a tickling sensation, but he knew better than to squirm. Fascinated with this new healing approach, Alana, Oliver, and Josie leaned in closer to witness the hummingbird's magic.

Opal blew a soft breeze of air and a low humming vibration into Long Shadow's ear. She continued the warm stream until the missing skin filled in and his dented shoulder rose like baked bread. Within a matter of seconds, his shoulder was whole, and the bleeding stopped.

Impressed with her seamless powers, Long Shadow lightheartedly asked, "Who needs a galactic portal when you have a magic hummingbird?"

"That. Was. Awesome." Josie's face momentarily resembled an awestruck kitten, really appreciating Opal in all of her splendor.

Not one for compliments, Opal continued her healing methods. "Lift up your shirt, Long Shadow."

Long Shadow lifted his shirt up to his neck and looked down at his chest area. They all looked at his upper torso with surprise. He was no longer tattooed. The Crow literally withdrew the ink from his body, and apparently whatever the ink was hiding.

Opal's head drooped to her chest and she muttered, "I should have known."

"Should have known what?" asked Long Shadow.

"They hid a spiritual key in the tattoo. Unbeknownst to us, that's how they accessed the Yellowstone dimension the night that we entered the Pentagon device." Opal lifted her head and continued, "But we still have the upper hand."

"How so?" my mother inquired.

"We completed our mission before they attacked the star. We found and secured Long Shadow before the Crow found us. And I memorized the musical key that unlocked their hidden location, within the red dimension. As of right now, they have no idea that we know of their whereabouts."

"Yeah, only if they didn't hear the Crow's strangled screams from a mile away," Long Shadow said in a serious voice.

"Well, how would we know?" Alana queried.

"We wouldn't," Opal responded, and then said, "Long Shadow, can you please hold still? I can seal your chest and upper torso so that the Sashimi cannot access you." Opal sang her familiar 'O' sound, focusing on his upper torso, where a faint swirl of glitter immersed with his skin. Zeke barked from under the couch, startling everybody in the room. We had forgotten about Zeke in all the commotion and directed magic. Opal flew up onto the chandelier, bracing herself for another attack. When it didn't come, she scowled at Zeke.

I shrugged and said, "Zeke likes glitter, oranges, and rainbow paths," as if that were the only suitable explanation for his sudden outburst. I reached under the couch and scooped up Zeke with renewed affection. He planted kisses on my nose, trying to heal the damage that Opal had just repaired.

Dad patted Zeke and changed the subject. "The Crow was saying something about dark matter dampening Josie's DNA. What's the point if we already completed the mission and aligned our universe with light?"

Still seated on the chandelier, looking weary, Opal responded, "Although we reversed the dampening, Josie was close to being harmonized with the black dimension. And the only reason they would go to such great lengths is if they planned on putting her back in the portal, to connect with HD140283."

"So, it sounds like you're saying Josie will always be in danger of being found and turned to the dark side, like one of those Jedi movies?" my dad asked with annoyance.

"Wait, why can't we just seal her the way you sealed Long Shadow?" my mother interjected.

"I did, I just didn't tell you. That's how Josie went into a deep sleep when the Crow's venom entered her blood. The light diverted the dark matter, but it stayed inside her body until I pulled it out." Opal sighed and said, "We need to attack the Sashimi's lair whilst we still have the element of surprise. Annihilating their headquarters is the only way to sever the head of the proverbial snake."

"If we destroy their base, then we won't have to live our lives looking over our shoulders?" my dad asked with hope.

"Correct," said Opal. She could sense we were finally starting to understand the truest gravity of the situation. "Might I make a suggestion?"

"Sure," I said, waiting for her to reveal another plan.

"I'm going to recommend all of us sleeping in the same

room for a brief nap. Consider it a recalibration. When we wake up, I think we'll all be energized and on the same page, ready for our re-entrance into the red dimension."

"Can you put us to sleep?" Long Shadow asked.

"Yes, and the sooner we nap the quicker we can awaken." Opal motioned toward the stairs and said, "Where Josie and Alana slept should be a big enough bedroom. Find a spot and get comfortable." Opal waited for them to exit the living room and walk upstairs before taking flight. She observed the area to make sure she wasn't missing anything.

Chapter 4

Mom and I made a beeline for the master bed, kicking off our shoes and snuggling with pillows. Dad draped himself across the loveseat, and Long Shadow sat in the recliner. We all looked at Opal expectantly, watching her glide onto the nightstand.

"Sweet dreams, everybody," Opal said. She opened her beak and sang a soothing melody. Within a matter of seconds, the environment was muted, and they dozed into a peaceful sleep. The first to awaken in the rainbow path was Opal, followed by my dad, Mom, Zeke and Long Shadow. The brilliant colors formed a tight circle around the bedroom, as if protecting us from outsiders.

"This is what we needed," my mom said, inhaling and exhaling the rainbow path's warmth.

Opal flew up to the ceiling, concentrating on the bed. They all followed her gaze and realized I was still asleep.

"Why isn't Josie awake?" my dad said with concern.

"That's a good question," said Opal, "and one I'm trying to figure out." She sang a chorus of different vowel sounds, activating each band of color from the rainbow path.

Zeke spoke and shocked all of them. "Josie's in another dimension," he said. "I can find her."

"Zeke, you speak!" My dad covered his nose and mouth with his hands, forming a diamond shape.

"How did she separate from us?" Opal quizzed Zeke, not sure if she should trust him.

"The Crow planted something in her hand." Zeke said and then licked his paw.

"What did he plant in her hand? And why didn't you use telepathy to alert me?" Opal seemed livid.

Zeke paused his licking and held Opal's glare before saying, "It was a piece of metal. I could smell it. It's the same kind of metal inside my body, when Mom and Dad took me to the vet's office. I think that's why I couldn't communicate, but I wanted to."

"Those evil, conniving Sashimi! The Crow put a microchip in her hand. He misled us when he said it was dark matter eating at her DNA. He knew I would be focused on withdrawing a liquid substance, and not searching for a technological device." Opal flew to the dresser, across from the bed, where she carefully considered the new information.

"This certainly changes things," my mom said.

"Right," Opal responded, "and Zeke is the only one who can get to her because he's chipped as well."

Zeke nodded his head. "I think if you find my chip's frequency and match it to Josie's then I can locate her."

Long Shadow scratched his head and looked at my Dad. "Has your dog always been this smart?"

"How would I know? I feel like I hardly know him at all." Dad smiled at Zeke.

Zeke responded by raising his little nose into the air and saying, "Hmph... Josie's my best friend. She knows all my tickle spots."

Mom laughed and then quickly recovered. "We love

you, Zeke. Please help us find Josie and bring her back to reality or the rainbow dimension."

"Actually," Opal said, "she needs to wake up in here, on the rainbow path, so she can feed from the rainbow's energy before we dimension jump."

"I'm ready," said Zeke.

"Yes, you are," Opal whispered with admiration. She opened her beak again and sang a low vowel sound, altering the pitch ever so slightly, in order to match the chip's frequency. When she found it, she made an imperceptible head nod, letting him know the next phase. Zeke closed his eyes and soon went unconscious. Opal continued the low vowel sound before opening another vocal pathway from inside her body. None of them had ever witnessed Opal singing with multiple voices. It was as though there were another bird in the room.

The second humming sound was a higher pitch that locked in with the low vowel sound, making a symphony of sorts. The result was a trembling of Zeke's and Josie's bodies, signifying their otherworldly alignment. Mom gasped, mesmerized at the strangeness of a dimension within a dimension.

She whispered to the room, "When this is all over, I'm going to kiss every inch of Zeke's body."

"Me, too," said Long Shadow. Dad scowled at his humor, indicating they should remain serious until sign of a positive outcome.

Chapter 5

Zeke drifted into a deeper sleep then he was accustomed to, unable to feel his limbs. A vision opened in his mind, where he could see a colorful cloud dancing on the horizon. Within the cloud was the outline of a distant land, a hill overlooking a lake. He could feel himself being pulled into the cloud and into another dimension. He gently landed at the top of the hill, where the landscape opened, and he could see an unobstructed view in either direction. What caught his attention were two solitary figures standing in the center of a lake. He immediately recognized Josie, but it took him a little longer to distinguish the second figure as Cilantra. Something was off with Cilantra; she was not herself.

Zeke barked, not liking the unease of the situation. *Where were they?* When he didn't receive a response, he made his way down the hill, and to the center of the lake. He looked up at Josie and Cilantra, who were involved in a heated discussion. Cilantra's face was contorted with anger – something he wasn't used to, since she had always been a pleasant guest at their home. But, then again, there was something strange about her scent; cold and malevolent. Zeke put himself between them, bracing himself to bite Cilantra's ankle if she lashed out at Josie.

"It's over!" screamed Cilantra. "You found the Sashimi and killed the Crow. Stop going on these crazy adventures. You're causing harm to the timeline!"

Josie yelled, "Cilantra, why are you here? You know that there's more to accomplish with Opal's help. If we stop now, then the Sashimi might retaliate. We can't let them have the upper hand!"

Zeke barked, interrupting their conversation, "Josie, this isn't Cilantra."

Josie looked down at Zeke, as if seeing him for the first time. "What are you talking about? And where did you come from?"

Zeke repeated himself, "This isn't Cilantra. It's the Crow."

Josie took a step backward, unsure of herself and what Zeke was saying. Cilantra stopped shouting and began to laugh. It was a maniacal laugh that segued into a high-pitched cackle. Cilantra's image disappeared and was replaced with the Crow's physique. The Crow started growing, taller and taller, entertained at their bewilderment.

"No," said Josie, sounding on the verge of tears.

Zeke sprang into action and shouted, "Run!"

Together, we ran to the hill and up to the cloud portal, which was still glinting its' existence. The Crow jumped and blocked our entrance. He swung at me with a claw, and sliced my arm clean off my body. I screamed and collapsed to the ground. Zeke was shocked and running on pure adrenaline. He knew if he didn't act quick then we might both be trapped in this dimension with the Crow. He mustered all his strength and willed himself to grow. That's all he could think of, was to grow, so that he could be on an even playing field with the Crow. And grow he did. Zeke shot up past the Crow's head, and without thinking, he swiped at the Crow's face with a gigantic paw. He sent the

Crow tumbling down the hill side.

Zeke didn't wait for a response. Instead, he knelt down and locked his jaws onto the back of my shirt. He willed himself to shrink small enough to fit through the portal, but still bigger than his original size. I was sobbing and hysterical as he dragged me into the rainbow dimension.

I sat up in bed screaming, "Noooooo!"

Mom jumped on top of me and hugged me from behind, "Josie, you're with us now. What's wrong, sweetie? Open your eyes, you're in the rainbow path."

I frantically opened my eyes and looked at my arms and hands, making sure I was intact. I hugged myself, my mom and then Zeke. "Thanks for saving me, Zeke." In response, he licked my hand to acknowledge what he had seen before dragging me into the rainbow dimension.

"I need a moment," I said.

Opal chimed in, "Zeke, what happened?"

Zeke sighed and said simply, "Everything happened so fast. When I entered the dimension where Josie was, I was on top of a hill looking at Josie and Cilantra arguing. But it wasn't Cilantra. I picked up on the Crow's scent. As soon as I identified him, he morphed into the Crow and grew about ten feet. We ran, but not before he sliced off one of Josie's arms. I forced myself to grow bigger than him so that I could fight. I knocked him out, grabbed Josie, and returned here."

"Josie, I'm so sorry," Opal said. "You warned us with your dream from last night, when you said there were two Cilantras. Unfortunately, you can never return to that alternate lake dimension, where the Crow sliced your arm. That's where the Crow can defeat you, since he's already drawn blood."

Opal paused, examining Josie's face, "This is my fault. I need to think two steps ahead of the Crow so that they can stop outmaneuvering us at every juncture."

The room remained silent whilst Opal thought of a solution. She paced back and forth on the dresser, plucking at her feathers. A few minutes passed, then Opal said, "I've got an idea."

Zeke perked up, waiting for Opal's instruction.

"We need to reverse engineer this and throw some decoys. Josie and Zeke, I'm going to put you under for about five minutes so I can realign the dimensions and the microchips. This time, if the Crow tries to access either of you, he'll be redirected to a place where the other hummingbirds can deal with him. He's no match for the rainbow path, and some of its alcoves." Without further explanation, Opal sang the vowel sounds in both voices, putting Zeke and I to sleep.

My parents barely had time to protest; they uttered "but—" and then Opal was waving a wing, insisting they hush so that she could carry on about her spiritual duties. Together, Zeke and I were transported inside a cloud, watching as electric sparks erupted like tinsel, reprogramming the portal openings. I could vaguely make out the lake dimension, where sparks were touching the top of the hill. It seemed like only a few seconds and then we reasserted ourselves into the rainbow path.

"That was quick," I said.

Dad put his head in his hands and sighed, "So many questions." He looked at Opal, pondering what to say next.

Mom spoke before he had a chance to continue.

"Alright, so the portals are closed. There's still the issue of the microchips. How do we extract those from Josie and Zeke?"

Opal responded, "It's the same concept as pulling out the dark liquid, but a little more difficult since we're dealing with technology. Josie's is probably still lodged in her hand, and can easily be pushed out of an open wound. However, Zeke's chip is probably embedded in his back, right?" Opal looked at Dad for confirmation.

Dad nodded, *yes*.

"To remove Zeke's chip, one of you will have to make an incision on his back, deep enough to provide a path. Then I can pull it out like a magnet."

"Will it be painful?" asked Long Shadow.

Opal considered. "Yes, but I think I can help. Before we do anything, I want each of us to relax and focus on our own vibration. As silly as it sounds, just start humming at different octaves until you activate one of the colors from the rainbow path. Once activated, allow the color to penetrate your spirit with healing and strength."

"Now?" Mom inquired.

"Yes, please. As per usual, we must make haste. I can only remove the chips in our reality. And we're pressed for time because we still need to make the trek into the Sashimi's lair. Any other questions?" Opal inquired.

"Nope, I'm good," said Long Shadow, who leaned back in the recliner and closed his eyes. We all followed suit, relaxing and humming at different intervals. It was an odd cacophony of melodies.

I activated the first color, perhaps because the rainbow path could sense my desperation to heal the psychological wounds. An orange stripe jumped up from the path and captured me in a bright bubble. My entire body seemed to melt into warmth and wholeness. I peeked through my eyes and could see other colors being activated; Mom was yellow, Dad was purple, Long Shadow was green, and Zeke was fuscia. I wasn't sure, but I thought I could see Opal smiling. She must have been proud of her spiritual pupils.

After some untold amount of time, the colors jumped from us and returned to the rainbow path. Opal waited a few seconds longer, then she sang a vowel sound. We all awoke in the bedroom, where I could once again feel my arms. Opal was still sitting on the dresser, observing our movements. She cleared her throat and reminded us of how quickly we needed to carry on with our mission.

"Welcome back, crew. We still have some challenges ahead of us." She motioned her wing in Josie's direction. "Josie, please put your hand on the dresser."

I slowly made my way from the bed to the dresser and looked at my hand, which was now swollen and tender.

"This will only hurt a tiny bit, more like a nudging sensation as the chip works its way out of the wound," Opal said with confidence. I nodded my understanding and stared intently at the bandaged wound, where the crow sliced my hand. Opal began singing and inhaling simultaneously, as though she were sucking in the chip. It worked! I could feel the chip moving along the underside of my skin, making its way to one of the claw marks on my hand. Opal stopped her singing and said, "Josie, peel back the bandage, pluck out the chip, and set it on the dresser."

I reached down and peeled the bandage off. I had to squint to see the microchip. It was miniscule, like the size of a grain of rice. I pinched it with my fingers and transitioned it onto the dresser. My dad, Mom, and Long Shadow all scooched in around me to get a look.

"It doesn't look like a microchip," said Dad.

"No, it looks like a grain of rice," Mom added.

"That was my exact thought," I said.

"Who is volunteering to make an incision in Zeke's back?" Opal asked the room.

"I'll do it," said Long Shadow. "It would be better if a non-family member inflicted a wound, right?"

"That makes sense," said Mom.

"Whew! I was worried I would have to do it," I confided. I looked at Zeke, who was calmly sitting at the edge of the bed. It was hard to tell if he could understand our conversation, or if his understanding was removed in this realm. Either way, he seemed to sense we were talking about him.

Long Shadow reached into his pocket and grabbed a small switchblade. He shrugged as if to say, '*I always carry one of these*,' then he looked at Opal for further instruction.

"Right," Opal said, "you'll need to sterilize that blade with rubbing alcohol." Long Shadow nodded in acknowledgment and made his way into the joined bathroom area. He found the alcohol and cotton balls under the sink and proceeded to cleanse the blade. When it was clean, he entered the bedroom with renewed purpose.

"Just make it a small incision," Opal said, "maybe one inch in length. Cut parallel to the spine, not on the spine."

Long Shadow was quick. He sat next to Zeke, patted him on the head, and said, "Try not to bite me."

I took that as my cue and sprang to action. I knelt in

front of Zeke and held his head steady, planting a smooch on his nose. I nodded at Long Shadow and he proceeded to pull Zeke's skin taught, making a fast incision along Zeke's spine.

Zeke yelped and squirmed. I released his head and let him attempt to lick his wound, but it was in a hard-to-reach place. Long Shadow stood up and wiped the blade with more alcohol and cotton balls. Opal asked, "Josie, can you please hold Zeke still whilst I sing and draw out the chip?"

"Of course," I said. I repositioned myself on the bed and put Zeke in my lap, clasping him between my arms. Opal commenced singing and inhaling. Zeke fidgeted because he could feel the chip working its way along his spine. He stopped when the microchip popped out of the opening, resting at the top of the wound. I picked it up and walked it over to the dresser. I set it next to the chip from my hand and noticed that Zeke's was a little bigger.

"Great," said Opal. "I intend to stay ahead of the Sashimi's movements by taking these chips and dropping them into a nearby lake. This way, if they're still tracking, then hopefully they'll teleport right into a lake."

"Will the chips malfunction if they enter water?" I asked.

"They shouldn't, but it wouldn't hurt to play it safe. Help me find something waterproof that we can put the chips in and launch into the lake," Opal implored.

Long Shadow stood up. "I saw something in the bathroom, a jar with a lid."

"That'll work," said Opal. Long Shadow went into the bathroom and retrieved the jar. After Opal dropped the chips into the jar, he tightened the opening and handed it back to her. Opal looked at him with another of her strange looks, "Would you like me to palm it?" she asked sarcastically.

Dad snorted and said, "Opal, I'll drive you to the nearest lake. Everybody else can stay here, in case the Sashimi try to show up."

Long Shadow laughed and said, "It's been a long couple of days." He handed the jar to Dad and then plopped into the recliner.

Dad and Opal left the house, with the chips, and the Crow's dead body. Dad texted thirty minutes later. *Mission complete*, he said. They found a lake about five miles down the road. They were on their way back, but not before Opal told him to relay a brief message – be ready to enter the ruby forest upon their return.

Chapter 6

We were all gathered in the living room, which was now a mess of feathers and Long Shadow's splatterings. Opal was standing in the middle of the coffee table. She pumped us up with a speech, something to the effect of us being a motley crew of degenerates and humanity's last hope. She really knew how to motivate us.

After reviewing instructions about what to expect, she paused and threw us a curve ball. "If my suspicions are correct, then the Sashimi have Cilantra hidden in their lair. That's how the Crow had the ability to appear in her form, in the lake dimension. Stay alert and let's see what we're dealing with." Before I could respond, she sang the hidden music note that was in Long Shadow's previous tattoo. The room dissipated and transitioned into the gorgeous ruby forest. Long Shadow hugged Zeke and observed the surrounding area. His first visit to the forest was fraught with tension, fighting the Crow, and he didn't really get a sense of the forest's majesty. It was stunningly beautiful. Perhaps with better circumstances he could enjoy the scenery, but right now they needed to accomplish a task.

Opal landed on Dad's shoulder. "The red universe was supposed to be a pure red universe, but according to the tattoo that was on Long Shadow's upper torso, the Sashimi have burrowed themselves down into a hidden lair. There isn't going to be a welcome sign, but this is the area the music note led us to, so we must be nearby." She looked around and said, "Just hold this spot. I'm going to sing and test the vibration of the surrounding area. Where there's Sashimi, there's darkness, and darkness has a different energy and vibration."

Opal began to sing in a hushed voice. Long Shadow could feel Zeke's heart beating with irregularity. He seemed a little anxious, so he gripped him tighter and ruffled the hair on his head. Opal finished singing and then stood still, cocking her head to one side as though listening or tuning her body into the environment.

"Over there," she said, "ten paces to your three o'clock." She jumped from Dad's shoulder and landed on the ground, which was covered with leaves. "Can you clear this area that I'm standing on?"

Mom and Dad reached down and swatted the leaves away, whilst Long Shadow held onto Zeke.

"What's that?" Dad asked, pointing to a small metallic disc. It was about the size of a dollar coin, painted black and flush with the ground.

"That would be their portal entry," said Opal. She climbed onto the metallic disc and tapped it once with her beak. "Hmm," she murmured, "if they're underground, then we could be walking into an ambush." She remained silent for a few seconds and considered a strategy.

"I'm going down first to assess the situation and see if I can figure out what's going on. You stay with Zeke and keep hidden amongst the trees. I'll be back with a summary of what we're getting ourselves into." Opal stood on the metallic disc and sang the same strange song that brought us to the ruby forest. She quickly vanished, leaving us to take cover behind a wall of trees.

Opal was instantly transported underground, where she found herself in a tunnel. However, it was no ordinary tunnel. The blackness was almost suffocating, other than the eccentric luminescent symbols lining the walls. The tunnel smelled like ancient decay, with a cold breeze that seemed to be coming from nowhere and everywhere. It would be disorienting for anybody other than the beings who created the tunnel, or animals who could use their directional senses.

She pressed forward and followed what could only be a large path. After beating her wings for what seemed like two minutes, she realized the symbols were doors. The tunnel probably formed a loop, with exit points at each of the symbols. That concerned Opal because there were a multitude of symbols that led to unknown rooms or dimensions. If Cilantra was here, then she would need Zeke to find her scent. He might not be a trained K9, but he was familiar with Cilantra. If anybody could find her, then he could.

Opal went to the starting point, near a long S symbol that was interwoven with spirals and loops. She sang the mysterious song, and nothing happened, nothing moved. She hadn't considered that there might be a different exit tune. She fluttered her little wings, thinking in midair. *Aha!* She remembered a previous encounter with a Sashimi from several centuries ago. At that time, she recited a phrase that was written backwards on a piece of paper, which opened an underground portal. The Sashimi were obsessed with mystical hideouts.

Opal gently sang the song backwards, following her

previously learned knowledge, and was transported back into the ruby forest, where the five of us were hunkered down behind trees. We flinched at her sudden arrival.

"I think I'm right," Opal said. "I can sense Cilantra's presence, but I can't make sense of the doors. Each doorway is protected with an unknown symbol. I need Zeke to help me track her."

Chapter 7

Opal made her way back up to Dad's shoulder, examining the area to make sure they weren't being observed. "What else was down there?" I asked.

"A circular tunnel with ancient wall etchings that led to other dimensions."

Long Shadow put his arm out to lean on a tree. He contemplated and then responded, "We're pretty exposed in this forest. If Zeke goes with you, then what should the rest of us do? Just tell me how and where to fight the Sashimi."

Opal gently responded, "I will tell you what I know, but we must be quick. Cilantra could be in serious danger.

"The Sashimi are evil but they're not smart. They rely heavily on tracking devices and technology that they steal from mankind. If they show up here it will probably be happenstance. Stay hidden as much as possible. In fact, I would find a pile of leaves and camouflage yourselves. If it comes to hand-to-hand combat, their eyes are vulnerable, more than human eyes. If you're outnumbered, do not run. Hold your position and try to negotiate. Make up a story about knowing where the yellow, black, and kaleidoscope stones are hiding. We can hope they haven't found them, and they never will. Just buy yourselves some time."

"Dumb savages. You want us to negotiate with dumb savages?" Dad said as he scratched his chin. Opal flew down from his shoulder and stood on Zeke's back. Zeke was unsure of what was unfolding and walked in a tight circle while nipping in Opal's general direction. She sang a quick tune to calm him down and keep him focused.

"Hopefully, it won't come to that," she said. "I'll be right back." She sang the Sashimi's entrance song. Zeke and Opal disappeared, leaving us to temporarily fend for ourselves.

As soon as they appeared in the underground tunnel Opal could sense Zeke's unease. Opal continued humming, directing Zeke to follow his nose. He suddenly understood that this was a rescue mission, first, and a destruction mission, second. They were looking for Cilantra, Josie's friend. He remembered her and his nose tingled with the familiarity of her scent. He continued walking until they stopped in front of a door with a large inscription above the entryway. It was a glowing Q with an extended tail that wrapped around the main letter.

"Is Cilantra in there, Zeke?" Opal asked quietly. Zeke snorted and belched with an affirmative response.

"Okay," she muttered to herself, "now to unlock the door. The letter Q with a tail wrapped around it – where have I seen this before?" She tilted her head to one side, considering a plethora of catalogued information within her mind. The answer was there, if she could just retrieve the context. She allowed her mind to wander until she landed upon a particular memory, from this century. She remembered hearing about a painting that was stolen from a museum. The painting was of a mysterious woman, only labeled as *Lady Q*. In the painting, the woman was wearing a long pearl necklace, draped around her torso and connected to a door lock. Upon further inspection, the woman was using the string of pearls as a key to unlock the door. *Pearls,* Opal thought, *something related to pearls.* This was harder than a brain teaser.

She continued with the thought process, aware of an urgent need to hurry up. She pushed herself to think hard - pearls come from clams, clams reside in water, water makes dripping and gurgling sounds. In Opal's experience, the Sashimi operated with sound as much as the other dimensions. Opal stared at the symbol and realized the Q's extended arm didn't just wrap around the letter, but also perched itself on the letter's back – almost reminiscent of a wing. *Okay, now we're getting somewhere,* she thought. *Maybe the Q represents a bird that makes a water sound?* It was a stretch, but like she explained to Long Shadow, the Sashimi weren't the smartest bunch.

The only animal in the world to make a dripping water sound was the Quarry bird, also known as the 'Brown Headed Cow Bird.' Sometimes humans lacked imagination when it came to naming things. Opal was familiar with the particular sound and began to mimic it. She was spot on and relieved when she noticed the Q glowing a blue color. A shimmering door appeared in front of them. Opal kept singing as she and Zeke walked to the other side.

Chapter 8

Opal was shocked with what she saw and exhaled with a grimace. They entered a large warehouse room filled with sleeping children strapped into wooden chairs. Hundreds of children. What were the Sashimi doing with those children? And how was she going to find Cilantra? Opal gave Zeke the command to sit still. She leapt off his back and flew to the ceiling. The room was dim, with poor lighting along the walls. There was a glowing device at the back of the room. It was moving in the same rhythm as the sleeping children. It felt like an eerie horror movie, where the villain lies in wait. For the first time in a long time, Opal's heart experienced palpitations as she considered the overwhelming sense of responsibility. She could not just find Cilantra and then leave all these kids here.

Opal forced herself to think of all possible scenarios that didn't involve torture or death, for herself or the room full of innocent lives. She started to form a plan as she looked around the room and noticed a tall triangle etching in one of the walls. That might be their next door on the proverbial path to find Cilantra. Opal was sure now, more than ever, that this is where Cilantra was located, if not in this room, then in the immediate vicinity. *How did the Sashimi pull Cilantra from the purple universe?* That would have been no small feat.

Opal flew toward the machine at a quick pace and

halted at what appeared to be a control panel. The levers were labeled with the same ancient Q hieroglyph, followed by a second letter of the mysterious ancient alphabet. Opal took a shortcut and touched the glass front with her beak. Instead of singing a song, she hummed a tune at a low volume. The device seemed to be controlling the seated children. Her intention was to connect with Cilantra, if she, too, were being controlled. If she wasn't in this room then maybe the device could inadvertently tell her the approximate location.

Opal closed her eyes and could see a transmitted scene from the next room. Cilantra was strapped on a table that was attached to a large mirror with glowing black lights.

"She needs to be awake for the portal jump," she could hear the Sashimi say.

"She'll wake up any minute now. We have time," said a taller Sashimi. His hair was platinum blonde, like the first one, but his was streaked with a black arrow. She would have to differentiate between them. She would call the shorter Sashimi Snausage, and she would call the taller Sashimi Torpedo Head. She learned over the years that comical names helped neutralize their projected fear.

Opal pulled her beak away from the glass and disconnected from the vision. She hovered in a defensive posture above the device, straining her neck searching for the hidden entryway to the next room. Behind a metal shelf she could just make out a small symbol protruding from the edge. It looked like a rod with a curved dagger. Much like the Mystery Q Lady, she had seen that symbol somewhere before.

It was four hundred years ago, in Bulgaria, where she

was fighting Sashimi. They shot at her and grazed one of her wings with an arrow, their weapon of choice. She hid in a cave, near a cliff, and waited for the Sashimi to leave.

They assumed she was dead, dropping several stories below, into raging ocean waters. In the setting sun, she caught sight of painted images on the cave wall. It was a pictograph, not as crude as cavemen drawings, but not as sophisticated as modern art.

There was an oval, surrounded with squiggly, radiating shapes. Above the oval were long lines, drawn at forty-degree angles, that seemed to be leading to a planet or solar system. Pointed at the oval was a painting of a short spear. The end of the spear wasn't a typical triangular shape but rather a curved dagger that was depicted with two blades. The only color in the pictograph was a dab of red paint, indicating spilled blood at the base of the oval.

Opal heard about the Sashimi's belief system. They used minors to infiltrate other dimensions and every now and then, universes. Their rudimentary practices involved ritual sacrifices, like many ancient tribes. Their ways were barbaric because their darkness literally and figuratively blinded them.

They were attempting to either sacrifice Cilantra or make her bleed, in order to connect with either the Pentagon device, HD140283, or both. Neither of those rituals was a viable option so long as Opal had anything to do with it.

Chapter 9

Opal formed a plan in her mind, reimagined it with several scenarios, and then cautiously approached the metal shelf. She touched the symbol with her beak and gently sang the opening song. She flew into the adjacent room with velocity and propelled herself straight up to the ceiling. The room's only light was coming from the oval mirror, providing plenty of shadows where she could remain hidden. Snausage sensed her presence and looked at the doorway, which was now opaque. He glared at the door and said, "I thought I saw something. I'll be right back."

Torpedo Head remained silent and stood at the head of the table, near the oval mirror. He nodded in silent approval then bent down and picked up a short spear that resembled the exact pictograph. "Take this with you," he said, and tossed the spear at his compadre.

Good, Opal thought. One less weapon to contend with. She knew she probably only had seconds, maybe minutes, before the departing Sashimi returned. She also realized that without the two of them rustling around the room, Torpedo Head would hear the fluttering of her wings. She quickly maneuvered above his head before diving down and driving her beak straight into the top of his skull. He reached up and tried to grab her before staggering and bumping into the table. He fell dead onto the ground. She narrowly escaped being crushed, but she could certainly hear (and feel) one of her bones break. There was a sharp pain in one of her wings.

Cilantra started to move on the table and opened her eyes. She was disoriented and alarmed when she realized she was physically incapable of shifting her arms and legs. Opal's beak was still embedded so she dug in with her feet and pushed. Her beak popped out with a grotesque suction sound. She quickly wiped her beak on the Sashimi's cloak and then called out to Cilantra.

"I'm down here, Cilantra! It's me, Opal." She tried flapping her wings to get up onto the table. The pain was extraordinary, and she floundered not more than an inch off the ground. "It would appear my wing is broken."

Cilantra turned her head and peered down at Opal. She was trying to speak but sounded groggy.

"Where am I?" she spluttered.

"We're inside the Sashimi's lair, underneath the red universe. We're in a hidden room and there's another Sashimi on his way back with a spear."

"Let me see if I can get out of these straps," she said as she rocked back and forth on the table. It was no use, she was temporarily stuck. She let out an exasperated sigh.

"I have an idea," Opal said and hopped across the floor to the oval mirror, "try to put your hand out with the palm facing up." Opal stood in front of the mirror and tapped the glass with her beak, until the bottom section shattered. She plucked up a shard, carefully positioned it in her beak, and then flicked her head in an upward motion. The piece of glass missed so she snapped up another shard. She hopped closer to the table and flicked it into Cilantra's open palm. Cilantra felt the glass and quickly closed her hand. No further instructions were needed as she began to slice into the leather straps. She freed her glass holding hand first, and then severed the remaining straps.

"What now?" she asked.

"Pick me up and put me on your shoulder so I can see what you see." Opal said as Cilantra bent down and scooped her up. Cilantra gently put Opal on her shoulder. Torpedo Head's blood was seeping across the floor. It would be the first thing his counterpart would notice upon reentering the room.

Think, Opal, think. "Alright, we need to get you to safety. Then I need to return and release all the children, and lead Zeke back to the portal opening. Those kids must be freed." She gave a little hop on Cilantra's shoulder and almost wobbled off. Opal looked at the mirror to see if the structure was sound. It was. She wasn't sure if her library of songs would work on this particular portal opening but it was worth a shot. She opened her beak to sing just as the Sashimi entered the room. She sang anyway, with just enough time to activate the portal. The mirror shimmered and the painted lights glowed.

"Hey, is that you singing?" Snausage stepped forward, slipped on the blood and finally noticed his colleague lying dead on the floor. Cilantra and Opal vanished just as they realized he was holding Zeke under one of his arms.

Cilantra's eyes widened upon seeing him but it was too late, they transported into the ruby forest log cabin.

"Stay here," said Opal sternly, "I have to alert the crew, rescue Zeke, save the children, and destroy the Sashimi's lair. We will all return here at some point or I will transport myself and contact you with further instructions."

Opal sang and reappeared in the ruby forest. She landed with a plop onto the ground, since one of her wings wasn't functioning. She didn't see the crew, as she affectionately thought of them, so she called out, "Josie! Where are you guys hiding?"

"Opal! Why are you down there? And where's Zeke?" Josie responded with quickness. The other faces emerged from the foliage at the commotion.

"Josie, Oliver, Alana, Long Shadow – gather around me quick. We're running out of time. I found Cilantra and transported her to the log cabin. Zeke was captured by one of the Sashimi, and there's an entire warehouse of sleeping children that need to be freed. During Cilantra's rescue, I broke one of my wings. I will need one of you to come with me, and the rest of you to stay put and guard this area."

Dad spoke first. "I'll go with you," he said.

"I'm going, too," I cried at the thought of Zeke being trapped with the Sashimi.

"No!" Mom shouted, "it's too dangerous of a mission. Stay here with Long Shadow and I."

Dad picked up Opal from the ground and put her on his shoulder. "Let's save Zeke and those children," he said with clarity and determination. Opal opened her beak and crooned the tune of the portal entrance. In a flash, they disappeared, leaving the crew behind in shock.

Dad and Opal re-emerged in the underground lair, outside the door with the Q symbol. "Stay alert," said Opal. "As soon as we enter, the Sashimi might be waiting for us. There isn't much light in the room, so try to hug the walls." With that, Opal made the Quarry bird's water drop sound, and they were able to walk through into the next room.

"What in the—" Dad started to say before Opal shushed him. He was astounded at the room of sleeping children. She could almost hear his heart breaking at the sight. She patted his shoulder with her good wing and then motioned for him to follow the wall to the back of the room.

"Head toward the glowing device," Opal whispered. Dad obeyed as instructed, carefully feeling his way along the edges of the room. He was trying not to focus on the children, who were strapped into chairs and motionless.

"Did I mention the Sashimi has a double-bladed dagger?" Opal said in a low tone. Dad stopped moving and she could feel his heart quicken. The vein on the side of his neck was bulging with fear. She heard the sound of dry spittle trying to make its' way down his throat.

"I can handle myself," he whispered. He resumed his course and finally reached the glowing device. "Now what?"

"Walk past the device to the bookshelf and stop," Opal instructed, "I have to sing another tune." Dad kept walking until he was standing in front of the bookshelf. Opal made haste and hummed her song, transporting them into the room with the Oval mirror. When they entered, Dad stepped in something sticky and almost slipped. He caught himself and braced his weight on the table.

"Oh no! We're too late," said Opal with despair in her voice, "Snausage and Zeke are gone. And Torpedo Head's body is gone. They must have jumped into another portal through the mirror."

"Snausage and Torpedo Head?" Dad inquired.

"That's what I named the Sashimi so that I can distinguish them. The Sashimi's devices are archaic. I'll need to smear some of Torpedo Head's blood onto the mirror to re-activate the portal opening and find their location. Hopefully, that will be enough to locate Zeke."

"Wait," Dad said, "What about the sleeping children?"

"The sleeping children are safe for now," Opal said, "but we don't know what the Sashimi intend to do with Zeke."

"No!" yelled Dad. This was the first time he argued with Opal and proverbially put his foot down. He continued, "Zeke would not want us to follow him knowing there are all these children that need to be saved. Either save these children or leave me behind."

Opal tilted her head and considered Dad's words. Finally, she said, "You're right. I let my emotions get the best of me. Zeke's like family. Let's return to the previous warehouse room and find a solution to transport these children out of the lair and into safety." Opal elicited a soft sound and they stepped into the adjoining room.

"I have an idea," Opal said. "Can you open the top of the device and place me inside?"

"Yes," said Dad, "right now?"

"In a minute. When you put me in, I'm going to sing a song that will break the trance and redirect these children to Carrington. Actually, I think we should transport them to Langdon field, where the local authorities can intervene and put them with their families. It shouldn't seem too odd, since Langdon field is notorious for vortexes.

"I'm going to transport you into Langdon field, with the children, where you will stay until help arrives. Make sure the authorities are alerted and that the Sashimi stay away from the kids. When you're done, seek shelter in your home. I'll come and find you as soon as I'm able."

"Alright, I'm tracking."

"Good, let's go," Opal said and pivoted toward the device. Dad placed his hands on either side of the machine and pulled in an upward motion. The lid lifted and Opal jumped into the water, making a small splash and plopping sound. She began singing with an intensity he hadn't heard before. The lights in the room brightened and then exploded, putting them in momentary darkness. Suddenly, the room filled with the feint outline of the rainbow path. It created a lasso around the children, just as they started to waken. In the blink of an eye, the room vanished, and they were all standing/sitting in the middle of Langdon field.

It was broad daylight and there was an elderly couple walking near where they appeared. The couple was startled and shouted, "Aaaaaah!" The older gentleman recovered first and pointed his cane at the sleeping children who were still sitting in wooden chairs.

"What are you doing with those children!?" cried the man.

Before Dad could respond, Opal bowed out gracefully and said, "I'll see you in a few!" She disappeared, but the elderly couple didn't notice. They were fixated on the scenario unfolding in front of them.

Chapter 10

Opal zapped herself into the ruby forest just as she could hear footsteps approaching in the distance. The soft crackling of leaves was growing louder. She scanned the horizon but didn't see the crew. "Alana, where are you guys?" Opal whispered.

From her left, a hand shot out, motioning for her to head in their direction. Opal bridged the gap and instructed them to touch her wing. She exclaimed, "Change of plans!" then hummed a vowel sound. She transported all of them into the underground lair. She realized the irony of them hiding from the Sashimi in their own fortress.

Opal didn't waste any time explaining the situation in as hurried a tone as she could, "Josie, Cilantra's safe in the ruby forest log cabin, and your dad is with the rescued children in Langdon field. He'll wait for us at your home once he finds the authorities. Zeke's been taken hostage by the Sashimi. I can track his whereabouts from one of their portal devices in the next room. However, it sounds like the Sashimi are hot on our trail. We have one opportunity to destroy this lair before the Sashimi can reclaim it. We have approximately two minutes to make the portal jump and permanently destroy this place."

"What should we do?" asked Long Shadow.

Opal continued her instructions. "Long Shadow, put me on your shoulder and run to the back of the room. I need you to destroy the glowing machine. Alana and Josie, run to the bookshelf in the corner. Knock it over so that the metal is touching the base of the glowing device, creating an electrical conduit." Within a matter of five seconds, they were all sprinting to their designated locations.

Long Shadow started with pulling out all the chords from the machine. As it began to whir, Opal jumped in and sang in those same two voices that she exhibited in the rainbow dimension. He could hear a slow thrumming sound coming from behind the wall. Opal tapped the glass with her beak and motioned with her good wing for Long Shadow to pull her out. He reached in with his hand and scooped her out like a toy in a vending machine. She coughed to clear her throat and said, "Quick, stand behind the bookshelf at that glowing symbol." Opal gestured with her head and neck to the hidden doorway, near where Alana and Josie maneuvered the shelf.

Long Shadow stepped over the shelf and linked arms with Alana and Josie. Opal pitched her tune and the doorway opened, propelling us in at a fast pace.

"Long Shadow, bend down and smear some of the Sashimi's blood onto your hand and then grasp the edge of the oval mirror. Alana and Josie, grab the other side of the mirror and don't let go. We've got one shot at a coordinated escape and explosion." Long Shadow did as instructed, his face a perfect canvas of stoic consternation. When everybody was in place, Opal released a series of multiple tones and vibrations, which sounded like three or four different voices.

The entire room vibrated, and then imploded just as we were sucked into the mirror. Opal picked up another chorus that carried us down a dark tunnel, and plopped us into a lake. We all submerged briefly and resurfaced gasping for air.

"Where's Opal?" I asked, still spitting up water.

"I don't know," said Long Shadow. He glanced at my mom.

"Josie, swim to shore," Mom said. She and Long Shadow dove underwater to search for Opal. I was devastated at the thought of our hummingbird drowning on such an important endeavor. Somehow, I managed to find the strength to swim to shore. I pulled myself onto the dry ground and then scanned the water's surface. My Mom and Long Shadow were nowhere to be seen.

Mom was the first to erupt from the water, holding Opal in her palm, above the water's crest. I could see her tiny silhouette. Long Shadow poked his head above the water and then lifted his arm with a thumbs up. They both started swimming toward the shoreline. Mom struggled a little, since swimming with one arm was a near impossible task. They both made it over to me, exhausted and sloppily trying to explain Opal's condition.

"She's not breathing," Mom spluttered and lake water sprayed in front of her.

Long Shadow crawled into a sitting position and then plucked Opal from Mom's hand. He gently pressed Opal's stomach with his pinky. She coughed and spat water in his face.

"Opal, please don't die on us. I don't know how to do CPR on a hummingbird." Opal turned her little head and spit up more water. When she was done clearing her airway, she launched a quick jibe at Long Shadow.

"That nose of yours wouldn't make it past my beak!" exclaimed Opal.

"I love you, too," said Long Shadow, pretending he was wounded.

In the distance, we could hear Zeke barking. We snapped back to attention and surveyed our surroundings.

"Well, our microchip in the lake plan ended up being more than we bargained for. We're near the lakehouse, this is where we ditched the Crow. It would appear the Sashimi tuned in to Josie's microchip, not realizing it was at the bottom of a lake."

"I'm just glad we found Zeke," I said wistfully.

"We found him, but now we have to save him from Snausage," said Opal. "Snausage?" Mom inquired.

"Yes, the short Sashimi's name is Snausage. I find that if you assign a ridiculous name, then the villain becomes less powerful. Anyway, he's the one who grabbed Zeke. And now we need to follow Zeke's barks and the Sashimi's footsteps. He's probably trying to find our makeshift headquarters."

"This saving the universe business is exhausting," Mom said as she wrung out her t-shirt.

Chapter 11

The four of us trekked through the woods and found a trail that led back to our safe location. We didn't dare speak, knowing that the Sashimi was out there and with our beloved Zeke. Which direction was he going? It's not like he knew where we were holed up. Maybe he was forcing Zeke to lead him to our hideout? So many thoughts.

About ½ mile along the trail, Zeke barked. He was probably a few yards in front of us. Opal chirped to get our attention. We gathered around Long Shadow and his dutiful shoulder.

"We need to flank the Sashimi. He's outnumbered, but he has a weapon. I'm pretty sure he's intent on stealing stones from Josie's backpack – we wouldn't want them falling into the wrong hands," Opal whispered.

"How do we flank Snausage?" asked Mom. I stifled a laugh.

"Josie, stay put on the back of the path. Alana, go right. Long Shadow, go left. Try to move in unison with the Sashimi's movements. Don't draw attention to yourselves in the woods. Alana, pass Snausage and then circle back. Confront him face to face but keep your distance. You'll distract him whilst Long Shadow clobbers him from behind."

"Be careful, Mom," I said in earnest.

We split our separate ways, making sure to keep our

footsteps as muted as possible. Mom was fast. She was confronting Snausage within a matter of minutes. Long Shadow let out an audible, "Crap!" as he quickened his walking pace into lunges.

Long Shadow emerged behind the Sashimi just as he swung at Mom with his spear. She jumped back and screamed in surprise. Long Shadow bent down and grabbed a thick branch. Without hesitation he brought the branch down on top of Snausage's head. There was an 'Oof' and then he dropped to the ground. He released Zeke's leash in the process. We were so happy to rescue Zeke and the feeling was reciprocated. He danced around in a circle, pretending he was chasing his tail. I picked him up and let him lick my face.

"What do we do with beef jerky?" Long Shadow asked.

"Remove Zeke's leash and tie him up," Opal responded. "I'll connect with the hummingbirds from the other universes as soon as we're inside our safe haven. They'll take care of him."

"We also need to figure out a plan to meet up with Oliver," Mom said as Long Shadow tied knots around Snausage's hands and feet. He stood up, examined the knots and then rethought his strategy. He pulled the Sashimi's unconscious body to the nearest tree, where he wrapped the excess leash around the trunk.

"This way, if he wakes up, he won't come looking for us," Long Shadow explained.

Opal was still perched on Long Shadow's shoulder and balancing herself each time he bent over. When he resumed his upright position, she continued speaking, "Yes, let's focus on getting back to the hiding spot. Along the path, we can discuss our rendezvous with Oliver. If I remember the drive out here, the path connects with the street parking. It's only another few yards around the bend, and then a quarter mile up the street."

Together, they walked and talked the entire way to the home. Apparently, Opal's abilities had increased since connecting with all the stones. She seemed sure she could transport us to Carrington, instead of taking the long way. We decided we would give it a go when we arrived at our log cabin.

We made it there without further drama. Once inside, Opal asked Long Shadow to put her on the kitchen counter and splint her wing. He found a small piece of wood outside, and a piece of yarn from one of the cushions. He carefully bandaged her wing, making sure he wasn't cutting off circulation. Opal nodded her approval and said, "I will need to put myself to sleep and heal my wing so that we can test the transport process. I'll also connect with the other universes and alert them to the unconscious Sashimi."

"No problem," Mom said, "is there anything we can do to help?"

"Yes, gather the stones and all our belongings. I think it's safe to return to Carrington now. Be ready when I awaken. There's no need to tarry here any longer," Opal said with tiredness seeping into her voice. She closed her eyes and hummed herself to sleep.

She was in slumber for about forty minutes, her itsy-bitsy chest barely puffing with air. If there was one thing that I learned about Opal, she was quick, fierce, and steadfast. There was no procrastination with Opal, it was either get in and fix the problem or get out the way and let somebody more capable fix the problem. I could tell Mom's countenance was strengthening just from being around Opal and absorbing her resoluteness.

We retrieved our belongings, including the stones, and set them in the kitchen. Long Shadow made an effort to clean up his blood and sweep out most of the feathers. Mom and I made up the rooms and beds. We were a little sad at the thought of leaving our hiding place. When we were ready, we returned downstairs and waited for Opal's consciousness to kick in.

When Opal opened her eyes, she lay still, drinking in the serenity of the daylight streaming from the kitchen windows. She jumped up onto her feet and shook herself free from any remaining droplets of water and dirt. The splint dislodged, allowing Opal to spread her healed wing. She flew up into the air, holding her position as long as possible until she tired and stood on the counter. Long Shadow clapped and said, "Look at you! Not bad for a self-healer." Mom and I laughed and then cheered for her recovery.

"We have all of our stuff," Mom jested. "If we're looking for a quick exit then we're good to go."

"Great," said Opal, "you know the drill, touch my wings and let's see if we can advance my transportation powers." We all happily minded her instructions, gently touching her wings until the room shifted and we appeared in our Carrington home.

"Wow!" exclaimed Josie, "that was the smoothest transition since the start of our journey."

Dad must have heard us from upstairs, where he was probably hiding from local authorities and/or Sashimi.

"Alana, Josie, Opal, Long Shadow! Did you find Zeke?" he yelled as he slid down the banister and into the foyer. He greeted each of us with a hug and kiss, including Long Shadow, who was accustomed to our displays of affection. Dad picked up Zeke and planted a smooch right between his eyes.

"There's been plenty of commotion here the past few hours," Dad said with a little bit of glee in his voice. He led us into the living room and turned on the television. There, in prime-time news, was Langdon field, covered with police, investigators, and neighbors. The title caption at the bottom of the screen read, *'Absurd Appearance of 107 Missing Children in Carrington County.'* Dad turned up the volume so we could hear what the Reporter was saying.

"Here, in Carrington County, officials are still baffled by what the neighbors describe as a miraculous appearance. One hundred and seven children, who were previously reported missing, turned up in Langdon field. Long known as a supernatural hotspot, Langdon field has experienced vortexes that have been reported since the 1950s.

"What's strangest about this story is how the children were found – strapped into wooden chairs. Investigators are still interviewing the victims and witnesses, but sources say they have already started contacting the families.

"Many of them have been reunited with loved ones. The remainder are staying at a local shelter, where they will continue receiving medical assistance." Dad bent down and turned off the TV. He looked at us and said, "How's that for a little poetic justice?"

Opal remained silent. I picked up on her melancholy mood and inquired, "What's the matter, Opal?"

"We almost forgot about Cilantra," she said quietly.

Her words were like a sharp knife cutting through the boisterous excitement. I immediately slapped my forehead. Mom and Dad looked at each other with their mouths agape.

"It's alright," said Opal. "I contacted her when I was sleeping and healing. I instructed her on how to exit the log cabin in the ruby forest, and transport herself to the purple dimension." Opal paused momentarily and then said, "she was sad that she didn't get to bid us farewell. The good news is that she was unharmed."

"In all of our adrenaline-fueled adventures, we were so engrossed in defeating the Sashimi that we forgot Cilantra was waiting to receive word that the lair was destroyed," Dad said.

"She will expect to connect with us tonight, as we sleep," Opal responded. "We'll all have our opportunity to describe our part of the journey and share with her."

"What's going to happen to Snausage?" I asked.

"Who?" Dad responded.

I quickly explained, "Opal renamed the Sashimi based on identifying features. She said whenever you rename a villain, then the villain becomes powerless – or something to that effect."

"To answer your question," Opal responded, "yes, something is going to happen to Snausage. I have no idea what the hummingbirds have in store for him, nor do I want to know. I've had my fill of mayhem and destruction." Long Shadow cleared his throat and interjected, "So, will I be heading back home tonight?"

"No," said Opal. "Stay here tonight. This is the perfect time to fit all the puzzle pieces together. I'll take you back in the morning."

"Is that alright with you?" He glanced at Mom and Dad, who were nodding their approval.

"Great," I said. "Is anybody else hungry?" My stomach was already growling just being in close proximity to the kitchen.

Chapter 12

That night was like a slumber party. We knew we defeated the Sashimi's core, and that they would be lost for quite some time. It was now up to the other universes to step in and hopefully, take care of the rest. We could gradually rejoin society and reclaim normalcy. So much of our journey would have to be explained over the course of days, weeks, months, and years. We went from a proverbial 0 – 200 mph in the span of a month.

I glanced at Opal throughout the night. There were times that she seemed as happy as we were, and times where she seemed withdrawn. There was obviously something on her mind, but she would only tell us in her own way and on her own timeline.

I was also thinking about our Cilantra connection. There were so many things I wanted to know about how she found herself temporarily in the Sashimi's lair, and how she returned to the purple universe from the ruby forest. Andrew was supposed to be Cilantra's protector, or warrior partner. *Did something happen to him?* It was comforting to know that Opal was protecting her and continuing her protection. It would be nice to see the look on her parents' faces when they watch the video greeting, from Yellowstone Park. They would be enthused to know how strong their daughter was in the purple realm.

After we ate our way through the food pantry, and

freezer selections, we headed upstairs. Opal was the first to retire for the evening. She flew into my room and nestled herself in the oversized cushions of the window seat. Dad activated the alarms and closed all the curtains. He was intent on all of us having a decent night of sleep. Mom made up the guest bedroom for Long Shadow, whose face was weary with the aftermath of injury and supernatural excitement. He shook Dad's hand and gave a little wave at Mom.

"Good night, crew." He patted me on the back before he entered the guest room.

"See you in a few," I said with a hint of teasing. *Would we ever actually sleep normally again?*

Mom and Dad retreated into their room and closed the door. I looked at Zeke, thankful for his companionship. He seemed to sense my gratitude and licked my pinky toe. I jumped onto my bed, whilst Zeke hunkered down in his favorite spot. "Good night, Zeke and Opal. I'm so glad you're on this journey with me." When there was no response, I looked at the corner of the room and noticed Opal was breathing heavily, apparently sound asleep.

Within a matter of minutes, I was also entering dream land.

It was such a gentle awakening that I hardly noticed a presence in my room. First, I smelled the soft scent of flowers. As I opened my eyes, purple light filtered in, making everything appear mysterious and majestic. Cilantra and a golden hummingbird were seated at the edge of my bed. I smiled and turned my head searching for Opal. As if sensing my desire to include Opal in our dreamscape, the golden hummingbird spoke, "I'm here from the gold universe. I understand you and your family have been going above and beyond to save all the universes and we are ever grateful. I thought you should know that Opal's earthly body is sick, and soon her time on earth will come to an end. She still has many things to show you, including the responsibility of the stones. You are not alone – I'm sure Opal will show you how to contact us." She paused and searched my face for a reaction. When there was none, she continued, "I realize it seems like an unfair burden, with Cilantra and Opal having to move on in different dimensions. The only words of comfort that I can offer you are this, the universal reboot and merge, with light, will happen sooner than you think – within your lifetime."

"I don't like it but I understand," I said.

"Very good," said the gold hummingbird. "You're entitled to your thoughts, emotions, and responses."

"Is it possible for Opal to transition into a human body and join our family until the merge occurs?" I spoke rapidly before she could squash my request. "Opal said she would love to be a part of our family. She's done so much for this realm. Isn't there something we can do to honor her wishes?"

The hummingbird thought about her words before she spoke. "It's possible. However, keep in mind, the priority has to be protecting the universes. Although the Sashimi's hidden lair was destroyed, they might try to regroup. Now that they are on the losing side of an ages long war, their desperation will cause them to lash out, and become unpredictable. You've got a piece of HD140283 inside of you. When you start to master the stones, your strength will keep them at bay."

"So, how long does Opal have?" I asked with trepidation.

"Long enough to make sure you're prepared," was the hummingbird's polite response. She flew to Opal's side and blew a tuft of air containing glitter. "That should hold her together for a while longer. As soon as I leave, she'll wake up. Is there anything else you would like to know?"

"Not that I can think of," I confided.

"Then, I'll be on my way. You, Cilantra, and Opal have plenty of socializing and strategizing this evening. Don't forget to wake up your parents and Long Shadow." She hovered above the window, casting a golden hue in the room's corner. The gold hummingbird vanished, leaving Cilantra and I to speak with Opal.

I crawled out from under the covers and hugged Cilantra. Opal awakened from sleep and joined us on the bed. It was so nice to see Cilantra, now that she was out of harm's way. Her dark brown hair radiated with a purple sheen from the room's bioluminescence. She looked like more of a teenager than a pre-pubescent kid. *Maybe these dimensions had a way of aging people?*

"I'm so happy to see you guys," I said with earnestness in my voice.

"Yeah, me too," said Cilantra.

Opal cleared her throat and said, "I suppose my buddy, the gold hummingbird, filled you two in about my need to ascend from this reality?"

"I'm really sad," I said on the verge of tears, "I didn't realize you were that wounded."

"It's not just the physical wounding. It's the fact that I've been earth's conduit for millennia. Although time moves differently throughout the universes and/or dimensions, a body can only survive if it's being nourished and healed. I don't plan on leaving anytime soon – there's plenty of magical work to accomplish."

"Josie, how are you holding up?" Cilantra inquired.

"I've been numb since the Sashimi's pier attack. The one time I allowed myself to feel emotions, I threw up on my shoes. And that was because I was so frustrated from the Sashimi's constant attacks."

"You guys did an amazing job finding me, saving those children, and destroying the underground lair. Not to mention closing the portal above Carrington, and coordinating a perfectly timed reboot of the universes." Cilantra patted my back and smiled.

"Speaking of the underground lair, how did they find you?" that was the question that I most wanted to ask.

"It was my fault. After we all left Yellowstone Park we went our separate ways. But the next day, I returned, because I wanted to enjoy a special moment. Our connection there was the closest I've felt to home since I left my earthly body. I didn't realize the Crow was there. He confronted me and then trapped me in a dark liquid bubble. The Sashimi arrived and they argued about what they were going to do with me. Eventually, they decided they would take me to their underground lair, where they would've sacrificed me if you hadn't intervened."

"I owe Zeke partial credit," Opal interjected.

I shuddered at what Cilantra said and then added, "My family would really like to see you. And you only briefly met Long Shadow, right?"

"No. I could only see him from a distance. I'm not sure

if he knew how to connect with us via sleep. And wasn't he awake, watching the tents?"

"Yes, I remember. He was a little freaked out at the appearance of the thunderbolt cloud. Either way, you should meet him. He's got a great sense of humor and he's been a huge help on our adventures." I realized just how much I'd grown to respect and admire Long Shadow. He felt like part of our family.

Opal flew to the ceiling and said, "I think I'll wake everybody up from here." She uttered a sweet 'A' sound and then returned to a sitting position on Cilantra's shoulder.

It was a full minute before we could hear my parents and Long Shadow stumbling down the hall, trying to find the source of the purple light. Dad knocked on my dream door and then realized he could just walk through. Mom and Long Shadow followed behind him.

When they spotted Cilantra, Mom and Dad immediately embraced her in a hug. Dad ruffled her hair and asked, "Did your parents ever see the video greeting?"

Cilantra turned her head and looked sideways at Opal. "Have they had a chance? So much has happened."

Opal chirped and said, "Actually, I was hoping we could visit them tonight. I think we can grace them with a beautiful dream. Why don't you all finish up here and then I'll go with Cilantra to her old home."

"Can we really?" Cilantra sounded excited. "I would love to surprise them!"

"Of course," said Opal. "You've earned it."

I turned to look at Long Shadow who was amused with our friendly nostalgia, even though he was an outsider. "Hey, Cilantra, I'd like you to meet Long Shadow. He's our friend and somewhat of a protector." Long Shadow smiled and extended his hand.

Cilantra shook it and said, "Any friend of Josie's is a friend of mine."

We spent the next hour (or spiritual equivalent) recapping most of the events from the past month. Cilantra was captivated with Long Shadow's retelling of the Yellowstone sweat lodge experience. And Dad was perturbed by her story about revisiting Yellowstone and being confronted by the Crow. Finally, Opal interrupted them and said, "We really should break away from the crew and allow Cilantra to visit with her family. I'll return as soon as Cilantra transitions into the purple realm."

We each said our goodbyes and watched as Cilantra and Opal walked out my bedroom window. I thought about telling Mom, Dad, and Long Shadow about Opal's injuries. I didn't because that felt too personal, and like something Opal should decide for herself. I didn't trust myself to speak about it without bursting into tears.

"Guys, Opal mentioned that she would train me with the stones. It sounds like there's a way to protect our home and family from further attacks." I hoped Opal was alright with me sharing this tidbit of information.

"That's fascinating, as long as the stones do not attract Sashimi," Dad said with a hint of sarcasm.

Mom swatted Dad's good arm. "Sweetie, that's great news. Don't mind Dad, he's a little tainted with hairy Sashimi experiences."

Long Shadow sat at my desk and changed the subject. "How will I stay connected with you guys? If I return home, the elders *might* believe me. It would be different speaking to them about everything we've been through. We have all experienced this journey together and should find a way to speak on a regular basis, if that's not too much to ask?"

"What's the saying? If there's a will, there's a way." Dad smiled and squeezed Mom's hand.

"Hey, where's Zeke?" I hung my torso off the side of the bed and peered underneath. At the sound of his name, Zeke raised his sleepy head from a pair of shoes. "Hi, Zeke!" He stood up and joined us near the desk. Long Shadow bent down and picked him up.

"Zeke's the only dog I've ever heard speak," Long Shadow said.

Mom laughed, "If only we could film him speaking and put him on YouTube. We'd make a fortune."

Zeke startled us and said, "If I could speak, then I would ask for orange flavored dog biscuits."

"What about peanut butter?" I asked.

"Yes."

Zeke was still getting the hang of this whole dialogue thing. This was the perfect opportunity to grill him about his likes and dislikes. "Do you like ice cream?"

Mom chuckled and added, "Or banana splits?"

"Yes."

"Blueberries?" Long Shadow asked.

"No."

Dad chimed in, "Steak?"

"Yes. Rare." We all laughed at his specific answer.

"Zeke, is there anything you would like to ask us?" Dad inquired.

"When I die, will you bury me with your remains? I love you. There's no other family I would ever want to be with."

The seriousness of Zeke's question was like a dagger to our collective hearts. It was so heartfelt that I burst into tears. Through my sobbing, I managed to say, "No more talking about death or the possibility of dying. I would be depressed. And yes, Zeke, I would keep you and then ask my children or friends to bury us together."

Dad grabbed Zeke from Long Shadow and then sat next to me on the bed, where Mom was already throwing her arms around me. We held each other in a group hug, releasing the anxiety of all our close calls and near misses. Pretty soon we were all crying. Even Long Shadow let slip a tear or two.

Opal reappeared in our room and quipped, "I'm gone for ten minutes and it's like a group therapy session."

"Zeke was just telling us how much he loves us," Mom responded and wiped away her tears.

Dad sat up, still holding all of us, and asked, "How did it go with Cilantra's family?"

Opal described their visit, "That was one of the purest and most special occasions I've ever witnessed. She was able to hug them and explain her new role in the spiritual realm. She also told them she didn't experience the pain of the Sashimi's attack. As soon as she said that, there was a tangible weight that lifted off their shoulders. I kept myself hidden, but she filled them in on the basics of our previous quests. She also said that your family would be stopping in to pay them a visit. They're excited at the thought of seeing Josie."

Long Shadow waited for a natural pause in the conversation. "What would you recommend we do next?

Should I stay here until the proverbial dust settles?"

"We would like it if you could spend a few extra days with us," Mom said. Dad nodded his head in agreement.

"Yes, let's talk about the next part of our adventure," Opal said with a lighthearted tone. "We've already gone on the offensive. Now, we need to focus on harnessing new powers and keeping each other safe."

"I figured you might want the zipper and stones back?" I asked.

"Those should stay here so you can make your home a fortress. The Carrington portal was closed and the Sashimi know better than to show up somewhere that has media coverage. They're desperate but they're not ready to take on the whole world. Your town is safe for a little while. We should all take advantage of this time to learn about the stones and how to properly use them." Opal tilted her head and continued, "Actually, I'm only training Josie but it's up to you to keep each other safe."

"Where will you be?" Mom asked with a puzzled expression. I cautiously glanced at Opal to see if she would say anything about her plans to depart this world.

"I'll stay with you as long as possible," was all Opal could manage to say.

"If I have a vote," Dad said, "then I say we use the next few days to decompress. Today's Thursday, so let's start with Josie's training on Monday. Also, I need to get permission to work from home for a while." Dad looked at Long Shadow and said, "You are more than welcome to stay with us as long as you would like. We will help you travel to Yellowstone, or maybe Opal can transport you whenever you're ready."

"That's very generous of you," Long Shadow responded. "Why don't we focus on one day at a time and get a sense of how things naturally progress?"

"I like the sound of that," said Mom.

"Well," said Opal, "now that that's taken care of, I have something special planned for us tonight." She plopped herself into the middle of the bed and whistled. I laughed aloud because it was the first time I heard her whistle instead of sing. She seemed amused that I laughed at her antics. "Prepare to be dazzled," Opal said with mischievousness in her voice.

Chapter 13

The room trembled with excitement and then a soft suction, at some unknown distance, was pulling our furniture and belongings toward the window. It was like we were experiencing a supernatural tsunami, where the waves (or air currents) race to the oncoming forces of nature. The entire back wall of our home became transparent. We could see a wave of rainbow colors heading straight for us.

I squeezed the covers and said, "Should we brace for impact?"

"Just enjoy the ride," said Opal.

The colors swept in and flooded the room, lifting up the bed and desk chair and carrying us into the open night sky. Within a matter of minutes, the constellations came to life and began dancing across the horizon. One of the constellations was holding a bow and arrow, which he shot up into space. When the arrow reached its destination, a rift occurred in space and the night canvas opened up. Behind our brilliant dark universe was a white universe, bursting with colors, sounds, and sensations. Their constellations jumped over onto our side and started dancing with earth's visible constellations. It was the most bizarre thing I'd ever seen and also the most magnificent.

We were all speechless and dumbfounded at the unfolding activities (and festivities). As I was watching the meshing of two worlds, the only thought that crossed my mind was, *this must be what the future merge will look like*. The rest of the crew must have been thinking it, too, because hope was written on their faces. We continued watching the galactic symphony – our eyes saturated with scene after scene of cosmic alignment.

At the conclusion, one of the constellations 'exited' the sky palette and shrank down to human size. He plucked a dancing flower from a nearby tree, walked up to Opal, and handed it to her. She was flattered and grabbed it with her beak. I don't know why but I started clapping, and then Mom, Dad, Long Shadow, and every living thing in our immediate environment, joined me. It was a round of applause for our tiny guide, Earth's true keeper of wisdom and our much-esteemed friend.

Chapter 14

The six of us spent the next three days having dance parties, eating humungous meals, and rehashing our stories. For the first time, Opal was relaxed and playful. Once, she even sat on Zeke's back and made whipping sounds. Zeke retaliated when he stole her food, and also when he sneezed in her face. The two of them were comical, like fussy siblings.

Long Shadow was pretty much inducted into our family tree. He looked at photo albums, watched family videos, and listened to our genealogical anecdotes. He wanted to know more about Mom's Brazilian ancestry, inquiring about the native population and customs. She was thrilled to have an audience.

Dad and I decided we would attempt a few drawings, or sketches, of some of our adventures. He was a natural artist, with an eye for the abstract. One of the first things he drew was a picture of our most recent cosmic adventure, during our rainbow path experience. He was enchanted with the way the constellations came to life, making the night sky their personal ballet. I had some of his drawing abilities and used his tools to create a charcoal sketch of Opal and I closing the portal, above Carrington. I filled in the spaces with colorful chalk, with the effect of a sharp watercolor painting.

On Sunday afternoon, Mom, Dad, and I decided we would visit Cilantra's family. We called ahead to make sure we would not be intruding. We invited Long Shadow, but he felt that it would be too overwhelming to explain his involvement. Besides, he was more keen on hanging out with Opal and Zeke. They were planning a field trip to the empty lot, where I first encountered the supernatural. A part of me wanted to go with them, but then I remembered how kind and loving Cilantra's family was. They would be ecstatic at our social call.

Mom baked a pie that we could bring with us. She was traditional in that sense, making sure that we were offering sweets to set their minds at ease. Dad cleaned up, shaved, and put on a button-down shirt with jeans. He had grown quite scraggly over the past few days. It was nice to see the normalized version of him… of all of us.

Cilantra's mom thrust open the door as we were making our way up the front porch stairs. She seemed brimming with exciting news (although, we already knew what it was). Cilantra's dad was standing in the hallway, with a big smile on his face. "We're so happy to see you! We've got some recent news," Isabel said. They welcomed us into their home and gave us each a big hug.

Mom handed her the pie and said, "I baked this for you, as an afternoon treat. Please tell us about your dream!" Dad quickly nudged her in the side and she corrected herself, "Please tell us about your news!" She realized that Cilantra's parents didn't know that they already knew about the dream.

Isabel gently took the pastry from us and walked into the kitchen. "How did you know it was a dream?" she asked.

"We dreamed about Cilantra," I said, "and we figured

she must have visited you, too."

Cilantra's dad said, "That's great news! It sounds like our little girl is making sure that we're healing from her absence."

"Yes, that's exactly right," Dad said.

"Please, have a seat." Isabel gestured at the kitchen table, "I'll serve us some pie with a glass of milk.

"Need a hand?" Mom asked.

"No, please make yourselves comfortable," she said as she flurried around the kitchen.

We seated ourselves next to Cilantra's dad. His eyes looked worn, from weeks of crying. His smile only intensified the previous sadness. Dad put his hand on his shoulder and said, "Before we begin, you should both know that we believe in the supernatural and spiritual. I know we've previously spoken about such matters, but we didn't really go into a lot of depth."

"I'm so glad you said that," her mom said, setting our plates and glasses in front of us. "We feel as though we have a better understanding, especially after Cilantra's visit."

Her dad raised his glass of milk, in a cheers salute, "it was three nights ago, when we were sound asleep. Our room filled with a purple luminescence, with the smell of fresh flowers. She and I both opened our eyes and were startled at a presence sitting on the edge of our bed. We sat up to get a better look, and were surprised at the sight of Cilantra. She leaned in and grabbed us both in a bear hug. I could feel the softness of her skin, and smell the familiar scent of vanilla and cinnamon." He waited for Isabel to be seated. "Sweetie, why don't you go ahead and finish the story?" He could tell she was anxious to talk about their dream visit.

Cilantra's mom continued, "There were the usual pleasantries. She asked how we were doing, considering all that had happened. But we were more interested in where she was and how she was visiting us. She told us about the day she died and how a magic hummingbird intervened to spare her pain. She said she immediately transitioned into a purple universe, where she's been ever since. She trains as a warrior, fighting dark forces and keeping balance in our realm. She also said that she's been working with your family to close the portal above Carrington."

Cilantra's dad interjected, "What we wanted to know was how she was in another universe and whether heaven was real?"

"Yes," said Isabel. "All of this is new to us. We just assumed she was in heaven, or some eternal resting place."

"What she said really changed our perception of the world and probably universe. She said there are multiple universes, and thus, multiple realities. Heaven is a construct of the gold and silver universes. In fact, the entire Abrahamic Bible and Sea Scrolls are from those same universes. Everything she was saying made so much sense, we just needed the explanation from an insider."

We continued speaking about Cilantra and her purple adventures over the course of three hours. We ate the pie, slurped up all the milk, and laughed until our bellies ached. It felt more like a celebration of life rather than a moratorium. Of course, we didn't tell them about the dangerous adventures, nor did we tell them about Cilantra's confrontation with the Crow. They said Cilantra could only visit them in their dreams, which was more than they ever bargained for.

At the end of the day, we bade them goodnight and hugged our way onto the front porch. Long Shadow was probably anxious for our return. Not to mention, Monday was going to be a big day with the stones training. Mom was planning a large meal and movie night, as the perfect segue.

Chapter 15

Monday morning arrived with the promise of a new chapter. Long Shadow was the first one awake. He sauntered downstairs and made a pot of coffee. As much as he missed his home, he was really enjoying his time with our family – he had said as much at our 'farewell' dinner. Opal joined him at the kitchen table.

"Good morning, Opal," he said with a brisk smile.

"Good morning," she said, as she groomed her feathers.

"I think I'll head out early and catch a ride with Oliver to the train station. I could use the extra down time and enjoy the scenic route."

"Long Shadow, you've been such an invaluable asset to this family, our world and the universes." Opal tilted her head and said, "It's been all action since your arrival, so it's been nice getting to know you these past few days."

"Will I hear from you again?" he asked.

"There's always the possibility of dream connections," she said and smiled. I entered the kitchen and caught their exchange.

"What's going on?" I said suspiciously. "Are you guys planning another adventure?"

"My shoulder says, no," Long Shadow responded. "I'll be heading to Yellowstone today. Opal assures me that we'll all connect again."

I went to the cupboard and grabbed the coffee cups,

putting four of them on the table. Next, I placed the creamer and sugar on the table, knowing that my parents would be joining us for breakfast. Long Shadow poured himself a cup and then poured some into my mug. "Cream? Sugar?" he asked.

"Yes, it's usually a little coffee with my cream and sugar." I laughed and poked Opal in her side, eliciting a stern chirp. "I'm playful but not that playful," she scolded.

Mom and Dad heard the commotion and came downstairs to join the conversation. Mom's hair was plastered to the side of her head, and there was an imprint of the pillow pattern on her face. Long Shadow laughed and said, "Nice hair."

"Shut it, dimples," was her response. We all laughed at her grumpiness. Indeed, Long Shadow had dimples on both cheeks. He was cute in a rugged kind of way.

"What's the plan?" Dad asked as he made himself a cup of coffee.

"Oliver, can you take me to the train station after we finish breakfast?"

"Sure, no problem," Dad responded.

We sat in the kitchen, making light conversation and drinking delicious coffee. Long Shadow was wearing one of Dad's outfits and offered to change before they drove to the station. Dad told him not to worry. He had a surplus of college sweaters and faded jeans.

Finally, Dad jumped up from the table and grabbed his keys, "I'm ready when you are."

Long Shadow hugged each of us, scratched Zeke's ear, and planted a kiss on the top of Opal's head. "May our paths cross again," he said simply. I felt an empty space in my stomach watching him walk out the door with Dad. Mom reached over and pulled me in for a hug. "We've been blessed to have known such great people in such a small amount of time."

Opal cleared her throat and said, "I thought we'd start today's lessons in the living room, with you and Oliver keeping a distance. How does that sound?" She was speaking in Alana's direction.

"I'm excited," Mom said. "We'll listen and let Josie ask all the important stuff. In the meantime, I'm going to get myself a shower and comfortable clothes."

"Speaking of shower, I think I'll bathe Zeke. He's smelling pretty ripe." I looked at Zeke who was sitting near the entryway, waiting for Dad's return.

I put my cup in the sink and picked Zeke up like a football, his favorite position. We all went upstairs, including Opal, who was coughing and chirping. About an hour later, we were all cleaned, and dressed. Opal made me fill the bathroom sink with water so she could give herself a bird bath. It was weird watching her perform such an animalistic chore.

I brought the bag of stones into the living room, where Mom was curled up reading a book. Dad returned from the airport and spotted us sitting on the couches. He plopped down into the recliner and Zeke jumped into his lap, with damp hair. Dad recoiled a little and then scratched him behind his ear.

"Long Shadow's on his way home," Dad said. "He's a good guy."

"Yeah, he's pretty cool. He'll definitely stay in touch and maybe even visit. I hope he has a safe journey home,"

I said, and then added, "Opal was about to start the lessons."

Opal was sitting on the table. "Yes, it's time to get back to business, so to speak. Oliver, Alana, the two of you are welcome and encouraged to stay and observe Josie's lessons. The things we're going to cover are applicable to all the universes, and your protection. If Josie alerts you to danger or senses the Sashimi's presence, then you can absolutely step in and assist."

"I like the sound of that," Mom said. She put her book down and looked at me. "Josie, as a reminder, school is about two weeks away from ending. I called your principal about an extension and she agreed that if you complete the exams online then you have completed your courses and can graduate."

"Woohoo!" I jumped in my seat.

"That will require some balance on your part, Josie and Opal. I realize that in the grand scheme of things school doesn't seem important, but it would look suspicious if Josie dropped out. We're fortunate she's already being homeschooled. Would it be possible to dedicate two hours of study time each morning, before training with the stones?" Dad looked at Opal and me.

"Yes, academics help exercise the brain. I think that's a good idea." Opal said, slightly amused that the girl who saved the world still had to finish homework.

Chapter 16

"Lesson one has to do with understanding the context of where the stones come from and how they were meant to be utilized," Opal started. "Each universe was created with a stone that came from the Creator. Inside the stone were the ingredients to life, as it pertained to that particular universe."

I raised my hand and interrupted, "Uh, have you met the Creator? Can you tell us more about that story?"

"In due time," Opal said impatiently. She carried on with the narrative. "The stones were activated, spawning the universes you interacted with. When the universes were created, the stones were deactivated, allowing a natural evolution to occur with minimal divine intervention. The hummingbirds were created as the stones' protectors, and thus, the guardians of each universe. We were not aware of one another's existence until about 5,000 years ago. We are the most ancient of all the creations, but not the most powerful.

"The story of how we all met was fascinating, but that's a tale for another day. Collectively, we decided that we would keep and hide the stones inside each of our own realms. Only the hummingbird would know the location. As the guardian of the kaleidoscope stone, or earth stone, I hid ours inside a hollow mountain. It remained guarded and well cared for until 2,000 years ago, when the Sashimi attacked the mountain. I fled with the stone and hid it inside a meteor that was just inside earth's galaxy. I figured the Sashimi wouldn't anticipate it being inside a moving target.

"The reason they pursued the kaleidoscope stone was twofold, in that it was a direct portal to earth and all its dimensions, as well as the master stone. It could absorb the powers of each of the stones. Keeping it hidden was of utmost priority.

"The plan worked until they started building starships. They figured out its approximate location and sent one of their ships to investigate. I sent the purple warriors to intervene, and during the battle they blew up the meteor. The rock where it was hidden careened to earth before I could stop it. What I didn't realize was that its trajectory was headed to Carrington, probably pulled by the yellow stone. I knew if the meteor crashed with the stone inside there was a possibility the stone might be damaged. In a rare move, I alerted the gold hummingbird, who said she would handle it.

"From your side of the discovery, it sounds like she sent one of the 'gods' to hide it in the abandoned lot until I could retrieve it. But, earth had other plans and sent you instead. I suspect the reason the kaleidoscope stone is so important is because it's not done creating. If I'm right, the stone will play a pivotal role when the universe completes its alignment." She paused to see if I had any questions.

My mind was racing with all kinds of thoughts. "Opal, why was the black universe created? Was it always evil? How were the Sashimi created? Where's the black hummingbird?"

Opal laughed. "I'd say those are pretty good questions.

I suppose we can speak about the black universe since we have the black stone." The expression on Mom's and Dad's faces were priceless. Opal switched positions from the table to the entertainment center and continued, "There's plenty of speculation about how the black universe evolved the way it did. Its hummingbird was the most powerful, with abilities that none of us had conquered. Our best guess is that it has to do with color and vibration. Unlike the other universes, there isn't as wide of a selection of black colors, or shades. Gray is not included in their universe, so their palette ends at charcoal black. The same with frequencies and vibrations – not a huge range. All of their power was condensed and intensified, since it wasn't evenly distributed amongst a broad spectrum. That kind of intensity exhibits in different ways, envy and hostility being amongst those attributes.

"The Sashimi were a product of that environment. They were using the black stone to bleed color into their universe and inject dark matter into ours. The kaleidoscope universe was, at one time, a kaleidoscope of colors and light. Then the Sashimi entered and altered this realm. At first, the balance was beneficial – the contrast seemed to make things more beautiful. As the dark matter increased, so did the chaos.

"At first, our realm didn't mind sprinkling color into the Sashimi's dark universe. But they never asked. They took and took and took, and then established lairs in the other universes.

"The black stone should never be used alone. It should always have a filter, or it should be utilized as a conduit. On rare occasions, it can be used to extract dark matter – like a magnet. Its true power is to complement and balance the other stones. Similar to the King Arthur story, only the pure of heart can tap into its potential and survive its strength. When the stone is utilized, it also becomes a beacon, attracting the Sashimi. You can use it in short bursts, but not an extended amount of time." Opal paused again waiting for my inquisitive mind to kick in.

"So, where's the black hummingbird now?" was the only thing I could think to ask.

"We ended his life yesterday." Opal stopped speaking for effect. "The hummingbird morphed into the Crow. He grew and became more vicious. He was a detriment to society and the universes."

"Will the Creator punish us for what we did?" I asked with concern.

"No. The Creator left us to our devices many moons ago," she said with abruptness.

"Oh, okay," I responded, not really sure if I should push the conversation down that path. Opal cleared her throat and then coughed onto the top of the entertainment center.

"Opal, are you feeling alright?" Dad asked.

"Yes, I'm fine. And it's time for us to speak about the yellow stone, and how it came to be such a hot potato!"

"Literally and figuratively," Mom snorted with sarcasm.

Opal continued, "It would seem intuitive if the white stone were the exact opposite of the black stone. And in some instances, it is. But with our creation story, the black stone's opposite would be yellow or gold. In addition to light, the yellow stone provides clarity. The yellow universe was attacked centuries ago because the Crow was convinced that if he could retain control of kaleidoscope, black, and yellow, then he would master all the universes. It wasn't long before he learned about other celestial bodies, creations, and devices that were a part of the bigger picture. Hostility tends to cloud judgment.

"They found the yellow stone hidden inside the yellow hummingbird. Needless to say, she barely escaped with her life. They relocated the stone to earth, in a volcanic area. As a side note, they enjoy chaos and hostile natural events, which seem to be happening more frequently these days. When they hid the stone, two things happened – the Native Americans were awakened to its presence, in 1805, and the Unicorns intervened to protect the entire area, in 1872. Those dates are significant because 1805 is when the Natives named the land as Yellowstone, and 1872 is when President Ulysses S. Grant established Yellowstone as a National Park. Those 3,000 miles started to become heavily patrolled and visited.

"At that time, the Sashimi were not aware of the Pentagon device. However, they knew the unicorns were responsible for awakening mankind, in subtle and clever ways. The Crow inscribed the stone with a unicorn's image and an arrow on its neck. As I mentioned, the Sashimi's weapon of choice are arrows. The Crow was essentially marking the unicorn as the Sashimi's enemy. The unicorns were unapologetic and continued to guide humanity through thoughts, dreams, and inspiration. When the military complex, also known as the Pentagon, was created in 1943, the Sashimi realized another force was at play. The hummingbirds were already apprised of what was going on, sensing earth's preparation for an alignment.

"Earth utilized the Natives to keep that stone safe, although they paid a heavy toll. And the unicorns utilized the U.S. military to protect the continent. If I might say so myself, the unicorns are absolute geniuses."

"That's a wild piece of history," I said scratching my head. I was shocked at the level of detail that was right in front of our noses the whole time. "Opal, where do the unicorns live?" I inquired.

In a tone that spoke of admiration and respect, she responded, "The unicorns live in the white universe. Unlike folklore, they are albino. However, when they interact with mankind they can absorb and refract colors."

"That's pretty cool," I replied.

"Yes, and so is the power of the yellow stone itself. It's the only stone that can calibrate and harness vibrations and frequencies. It can separate, unite, and clarify sounds and vibrations. Considering that every living thing in the known universe has a detectable signature, I would say that's a powerful stone."

"How should I use the stones to protect and defend?" I asked.

"Excellent question! If utilized correctly, then you should be able to camouflage with the kaleidoscope stone, hide or change your vibrations with the yellow stone, and deflect the Sashimi's power with the black stone."

"You make it sound so easy," I whined.

"Kind of. Remember, your DNA merged with HD140283. I have a feeling these will be minimal efforts, thanks to your genetic structure."

I raised my hand in a playful manner, "when can we start?"

"Let's start this morning. Pull out the yellow stone and set it in the palm of your hand."

With eagerness, I reached into the bag and retrieved the yellow stone. As it was sitting in my palm, I gently felt the outline of the unicorn etching.

"I have to start by calibrating the three stones, individually, so that they respond only to a set criteria. I will program the yellow stone to recognize your DNA. This way, if it senses dark matter within ten feet of you, then it will automatically cover you with a vibration that repels the Sashimi. I will also program it to camouflage you, your homes, and your vehicles. When it's programmed then you should be able to delegate those powers to a much wider extent. Basically, your DNA, within your body, controls these stones. Understand?"

"Yes, I think so."

Opal lifted her head and sang a warbly tune. I could feel a tingly sensation course throughout my veins. Mom, Dad and Zeke must have felt some residual vibration because they squirmed in their seats. Opal continued singing for a few minutes until the stone started to glow.

When she stopped, I interjected, "why didn't we activate the yellow stone sooner?"

"Because that device in the Sashimi's lair wasn't just putting kids in trances. It was tracking the stones and using children to connect with various access points. If we tried calibrating before we destroyed the lair, then we would have risked calibrating with all those children, whose DNA is not equipped."

"But aren't there other lairs?" I remembered her mentioning different hiding places.

"Yes. The lair we destroyed was in the red universe, the highest vibration, and the source of their efforts." Opal quickly glanced around the room and said, "Josie, point the stone at the plant in the corner of the room."

I pointed it like she asked. "Very good," she said, "next, put your mouth on the stone and hum until the plant responds."

"Huh?" I asked, "how will I know if the plant responds?" "Trust me, you'll know."

I placed my chin in my palm and started humming. Nothing happened. Opal patiently explained, "Try and fluctuate the humming, from high to low and then back again. Pay attention to what note you're at when the plant responds. Green and brown have a combined vibration. You'll get the hang of it and soon it will be intuitive."

"Awesome," I said and then started humming as she instructed. I kept at it until I felt the stone pulsate. *The plant was responding*! I made a mental note of the sound and stopped. "I felt the stone pulsing!" I shouted.

"You see? Nothing to it at all," Opal reassured. "You're ahead of the curve. This is a good stopping point. Your assignment today is to get acquainted with as many vibrations as possible. Tomorrow, I will teach you how to reverse and change the vibrations."

Opal flew down from the entertainment center and perched herself on the fireplace mantle.

Mom said, "I'm impressed. Also, I thought the book I was reading was entertaining, but everything Opal just described was beyond my imagination." She smiled and quietly clapped her hands.

"To celebrate," Dad said, "let's find ourselves a

science-fiction movie so we can yell at the actors and tell them they've got it all wrong, like Mystery Science Theatre." I laughed at Dad's weird sense of humor. "Can you hand me the remote from on top of the entertainment center?" he asked.

"Yes, and then I'll make popcorn." I walked to the entertainment center and reached for the remote. I stopped when I noticed a splatter of blood. That was where Opal coughed. *Uh-oh, I thought. How much longer would she be with us?* I tossed the remote to Dad in the recliner and exited the room to make popcorn.

Chapter 18

I paused my reminiscing and focused on the present, when I heard a noise coming from the tree line.

"Hello?" I called out.

When there was no response, I pulled the scarf around my shoulders. The hot apple cider was now warm, and teetering on the brink of cool. The sun was starting to set and I hadn't eaten anything today. My taste buds weren't the same as twenty years ago, resulting in a decreased appetite.

I remembered those lesson days with a certain fondness. I did end up passing my academic exams and dedicating all my time and effort to understanding and utilizing the stones. Although Opal calibrated all three of the stones, I barely touched the black stone. Opal said not to expose it whilst in defense mode. If an urgent situation arose, then I should only use it to extract dark matter or deflect the Sashimi's power.

All the excitement and grandeur of the stones wore off when Opal passed away. It was a brisk autumn evening when the leaves just started changing colors. We were seated around the dining table, finishing our meal, when Opal announced she was going to bed early. She referred to the window seat as her bed.

I followed her upstairs and crawled under the covers because I was worried about the increased instances of blood splatter. She wouldn't speak to me about it and she seemed agitated whenever I implored for an update. I brought Zeke up onto the bed and gave him a goodnight hug. He could sense something was wrong with Opal, so he jumped down and walked to the window seat. He raised his head to sniff the air. "Good night, Zeke," Opal said from between the cushions.

After reaching a nice deep sleep, I was awakened with the rainbow path entering my room. The gold hummingbird flew through the window and waited for Opal to rouse. Opal stood up and spread her wings, as if making sure they were still attached.

"Are you ready, my old friend?"

Opal glanced in my direction and noticed I was awake. I was leaning forward to hear their conversation. "Yes, give us a minute to say our goodbyes," she responded in a solemn voice. Zeke was also alert and looking around the room to figure out if he should stay quiet or greet the new hummingbird.

"Josie, it's time for me to go," Opal said, "but this isn't a permanent goodbye. We will still interact with one another in the spiritual realms."

I couldn't speak because the tears were flowing down my cheeks. It wasn't as if this day was a surprise, especially with how often Opal was coughing up blood. "Please don't go," I begged. It was all I could manage to say.

Opal left the window seat and perched herself on my shoulder, where she leaned in and poked my cheek with a gentle kiss. "I will always love and remember you and your family. I heard about your request on my behalf, and if I can make that happen then trust that I will be back in a physical body."

The gold hummingbird spoke, "Josie, we are all indebted to you. Keep yourself humble and stay sharp. We really must be going."

She started singing a melodious tune until Zeke interrupted and said, "Opal, you're the best. I like the way you scratch my tummy."

Opal visibly wept at Zeke's genuineness. Her little body spasmed as she sobbed. "Let's go, before I lose my nerve," she whispered to the gold hummingbird. She resumed her chorus and the rainbow path wrapped them up in light (and glitter), whisking them away to one of the other universes.

Zeke jumped onto the bed and curled up in my lap. We both let our tears roll until we transitioned back into our reality. I was too afraid to crawl out of bed and check on Opal's body. Zeke was already at the bottom of the window seat and whining. He stood up on his hind legs to see if he could nudge Opal.

Reluctantly, I pulled back the covers and glided out of the bed. I felt lightheaded and there was a hollow sensation in my stomach. *Could this really be happening? Were we on our own now?* I stepped nearer to the window seat feeling as though I were still in a dreamscape. I could see Opal's body, still curled between two pillows. I gently touched her belly and knew immediately that she was dead. She didn't respond. She didn't breathe. She didn't laugh at me touching her sensitive stomach. It was over.

I knelt on the floor, in front of her body, and wept. Zeke continued his high pitch whining. After a few minutes, I decided I would let my parents know. I exited my bedroom and knocked on their door.

"Josie, is that you?" my Mom called out with concern.

I opened the door and turned on the light. Mom and Dad sat up in bed and then saw the look on my face. "What is it? What's wrong, sweetie?" Dad was starting to dislodge himself from the multitude of covers.

"Opal's gone," was all I managed to say before almost collapsing.

"Where'd she go?" my Mom asked with a confused look on her face.

"No, she's gone. She left this world. We're all alone now." I could barely speak through the sobbing.

"Oh, no!" cried Mom. She left the bed and ran to my room. She turned on the light and made a beeline to the window seat. She touched Opal's wing and confirmed.

"Oliver!" she yelled. Dad was already running past me into the hallway. He entered my bedroom and could see Opal lying lifeless between the cushions. Dad pivoted and walked back to his room, grabbed me in an embrace and walked me over to the window seat. He hugged both of us on either side.

"Opal's not entirely gone," he said with sincerity, "she always talked about visiting us in our sleep and connecting on the rainbow path."

"I'm gonna miss her," Mom said.

"Me, too," I muttered.

"Should we bury her?" I asked.

"I think that would be the right thing to do, but not before I make her a bird coffin. I'm an architect, remember?" Dad said with a smile on his face, "C'mon, guys. Opal would want us to celebrate her life. She's one of the ancients! If she moved on from this world, then I'm sure it's for good reason. Maybe earth is no longer in danger."

"I hadn't thought about that," I confided.

Dad released his grip and said, "I'll start on the coffin right away. I've got spare wood and plenty of tools in the garage. Alana, pull yourself together and call Long Shadow. Give him a heads up and ask him to contact us if he dreams about Opal. Josie, if you're up to it, I'd like you to write a poem and pull together all your sketches. We'll make a nice tribute to honor her life and contributions." He realized he'd been a little harsh with Mom, so he hugged her and said, "Sorry, take all the time you need. I'll meet you guys in the living room in a few hours."

Chapter 17

My thoughts about Opal's burial preparations were interrupted at the rustling sound from the nearest bushes. "Hello? I can hear you, whoever you are," I called out in a stern voice.

"Josie," came a soft response.

I stood up with a quickness, causing my old bones to creek and pop. I definitely heard my name. The bushes rustled again, and this time, a slender woman emerged. She was a black woman with long grey hair.

"Josie?" There was an inquisitive tone as she stepped forward to examine my face.

"Yes, who are you?" I responded with a calm voice.

"It's me, Opal," she clasped her hands together and searched my face for recognition.

There were pins in my peripheral vision and I felt like I might pass out. I grabbed the armrest to steady myself, spilling apple cider in the process.

"No, it can't be. After all this time? Is it really you?" I squinted and addressed her in as calm and friendly a voice as I could muster.

"Yes." She sauntered toward me, ready to catch me if I passed out. She helped me set the glass of cider onto the wicker table. Then she gently pulled me in for an embrace.

"I recognize your voice. I'm surprised that you're in human form." I hugged her with all my strength and said,

"Opal, I've missed you so much. Time has marched on in our world, but I've always enjoyed our spiritual connections."

"Is anybody else alive?" Opal asked carefully.

"No, I'm the last one of our crew. And I'm barely hanging on." I chuckled at the absurdity of the situation. "In fact, I was sitting outside reminiscing about our last adventures. How did you know I was thinking about you?"

"Good timing," she said, with a sparkle in her eye. "Why don't you have a seat?"

"Of course," I tenderly took my seat, making sure not to strain my back. Opal sat next to me and held my hand.

"I'm here with good news. I'm allowed to stay with you until the universal alignment takes effect. It's really happening, and sooner than you think. I'm sorry I couldn't be here for the passing of your parents, Long Shadow, Cilantra's parents, and Zeke. You were all my family." A tear slid down her cheek.

I squeezed her hand and said, "It's alright, Opal. Time heals most old wounds. I buried Zeke with my parents on a plot of land not far from here. That's where I reserved a spot for myself. You're in there, too," I laughed, "like one big happy family. I dedicated my basement to a celebration of everybody's lives – there's pictures, drawings, poetry, and memorabilia."

"That's wonderful, Josie." Opal still sounded wise.

"If you're here to stay, then I do hope that you'll be my guest. I'm sure you recognize this as Maxime's home? I bought it from Stewart about fifteen years ago. He had been trying to sell it prior to his mother's death, but his mother's murder spooked all the prospects. He decided to keep the home and move his family in until they could make other arrangements. That's when I stepped in and made an offer." I shifted in my seat and looked at Opal's eyes. "Tell me the pain and sadness will all be over soon. Will we be united with our loved ones and celebrating?"

"Some things should remain a surprise," she said, with a hint of teasing in her voice. "All I can tell you is that it was all worth it." We sat in silence a moment longer.

Finally, Opal asked, "Did you manage to find a husband and/or procreate? I always pictured you a happy wife and mother. You have such a nurturing personality."

"Ha!" I laughed. "Yes, I was married forty years to a saint. He put up with me and all the crazy talk about other dimensions and universes. He was a true believer. He passed away just last year. This was our favorite spot to watch nature and romanticize about the past."

Opal could tell I was avoiding the topic about children and decided not to push.

I changed the subject. "Let's go inside and I'll show you the guest bedroom. If you're hungry then I can make a simple dinner."

"I would like that," she said. Together, we hobbled up the walkway, like two peas in a pod, and entered my home.

We spent the next few days looking at all the pictures and trinkets from our journeys. We laughed, cried, yelled, and comforted. Above all else, I wanted to know what she'd been up to since passing from our world. I pestered her until she finally caved.

"All I can say is that each of the hummingbirds had a role in deciding how events would unfold in this realm. We vanquished the Sashimi. And we found the remainder of the lairs."

"That's all?" I asked with sarcasm. Opal always laughed at my wit.

"Yes, that's the gist of it," she responded.

The remainder of our time together allowed us to bond, like sisters. As much as I harassed her for more information about the other universes, she kept silent. Instead, I relinquished some of my own stories. I confided to her that I used the portal zipper to interact with the universes, but only from the safety of the empty property next to our home. I was intent on describing every detail of the intervening fifty years.

Similar to the pier outings with my deceased husband, Opal and I walked to the dock in our backyard, before sunset each day. We would sit in the wicker seats and drink our cider, coffee, or tea. We were constantly laughing about our crew's ability to find humor in every circumstance, where appropriate. I also filled her in on my high school graduation, college graduation, first kiss, first date, first concert, and every other memorable event that occurred throughout my life.

On a cool Sunday afternoon, we followed our routine and basked in the glorious weather. We were now speaking about time travel and major technological accomplishments. There were plenty of conspiracy theories to keep us entertained. Although I was old, my mind was still sharp, thanks to the help of the stones. I was explaining quantum computing, or trying to, when Opal turned to me with a look of astonishment.

"Are you ready?" she asked simply.

"Yes and no," I said. The only thing that would

suddenly astonish her would be the much anticipated merging of universes. I said yes, because I was ready spiritually. I said no, because I wasn't ready physically. An overload of excitement might cause a heart attack.

As it turned out, there was no need to panic. Opal cupped my face in her hands and planted a kiss on my crooked nose. She carefully turned my head so that I could look in the direction of the setting sun.

I could already hear a rumbling sound. The ground began to tremble, and a gold light erupted above us. I yelled with vigor, "This is happening! Yes!"

Opal squeezed my hand and laughed. There, on the horizon, galloping along the skyline, was a herd of brilliant white unicorns. Their horns were attracting beams of light. They were coming at us from every direction. The birds began chattering amongst themselves in a crescendo of chirps and whistles. It was then that I noticed the perfect heart formation of hummingbirds emerging above the treetops.

The world was about to change.